QUEEN OF SPADES

AN EVA SANTELLA THRILLER
BOOK 1

KRISTI BELCAMINO

LIQUID MIND PUBLISHING

QUEEN OF SPADES SERIES

Enjoying the Queen of Spades Thriller Series? Scan the QR code below to order more books today!

Queen of Spades

One-Eyed Jack

The Suicide King

The Ace of Clubs

The Joker

The Wild Card

High Stakes

Poker Face

PROLOGUE

Do you like to play cards?"

He froze at the sound of the silky voice behind him. Only he could detect the slight accent. But then again, he'd known her since they were children.

"Vincenzo, I asked you a question."

His name on her lips turned his face icy cold.

Her spicy, exotic perfume filled his airways as she drew near. She moved closer stealthily, silently. The only indication that she was directly behind him now was a slight disturbance in the air and that heady scent filling his nostrils. He fought against the desire to inhale deeply. Just as he'd fought against his attraction to her the past year. How many times had she innocently brushed by him and he'd been caught up in the smell of her perfume. How many times had he tried to recapture Eva's unique and elusive scent in his memory. It was a fragrance he'd never smelled on another woman—and he'd smelled his fair share of perfumes over the years—from cheap drugstore sprays to customized parfums designed in Paris. This scent was difficult to identify. If he'd ever smelled it on someone else, Eva's inimitable chemistry had transformed it into something intoxicating.

He felt the cool steel on his neck at the same moment she pressed

. . .

HER WARM BODY fully against him from behind. Even as he felt the icy fingers of death race down his spine, he was aroused. That lush body pressed up against him and the cloud of her scent sent an ache of desire rippling through him. A lust he'd kept at bay, even refusing to acknowledge it to himself. Now, he let himself feel it and inhaled deeply, closing his eyes against the candlelight.

Then he smelled something else—something emanating from her pores. He paused. It wasn't fear. No. Nervousness? No. It wasn't that, either.

It was excitement.

But not the same thrill he felt in his groin. It was not sexual. This was blood lust. This was eagerness. This was her anticipation of the delicate glide of metal across his neck, carving into his flesh. He knew it. He recognized it. After all, he'd felt it himself. It was much, much stronger than pure sexual desire.

As he thought this, his own ripple of fleeting desire was quickly extinguished. He had to think. He had to say something to stop her murderous vengeance.

A silken lock of her hair brushed his cheek, and he squirmed in a mix of pleasure and terror.

"I don't know about you," she whispered, her breath hot in his ear. Her voice was low, husky, mesmerizing. "But I love playing cards. I bet you can guess which card is my favorite?"

The queen of spades. As soon as he thought the words, a white-hot bolt of pain raced across his neck, from his left ear to his right. He cried out in anguish, but there came only a thick gurgle and a small exhalation.

His last thought as he watched his own blood spurt wildly onto the table in front of him was that the crazy old woman on the sidewalk had been right —he'd never see the likes of heaven.

1

Eva White tried to sneak a look at her cell phone beneath the table but her downward glance didn't escape the Queen Bee at the front of the class running the parent volunteer meeting.

"Mrs. White?"

"Yes?" Eva jerked her eyes up.

"I think you would be a great candidate to head up the committee organizing the food drive."

Eva pushed down her revulsion at the woman's sickly sweet tone and plastered a smile on her face. "I think you're right. Food drives are near and dear to my heart."

It wasn't a lie. Back in Sicily, she'd made sure nobody who lived in her village ever went hungry.

"Wonderful," Krystal said. "I'll mark you down as chair. Remember, for every dollar donated to the Santa Monica food shelf, Tilly Conway's mother will match it with an equal donation to our school fundraiser."

It was a totally messed up way to raise money, but if it meant that a Los Angeles food shelf was able to benefit from some of the wealthy families in the school—even in a convoluted way—Eva was all for it. She'd hacked into Krystal's bank account last year just to make sure the woman wasn't depositing most of the fundraising money into her own account but, surprisingly, all the money raised went straight back to the school.

"So, I can count on you?" Krystal asked.

Eva nodded.

"You are now the food drive chair."

"Fantastic," Eva said, matching the blonde woman's fake excited tone. "And Matthew and I will match the food donations, as well."

Krystal beamed. "That's so generous of you."

But Eva wasn't done speaking. "But I think in our case, we'll match the donation with an equal one that will also go to the food shelf."

"That's a brilliant idea!" Nikos said. He was one of the dad's Eva had become friendly with over the past year. His son, Ricardo, was a sweet kid.

Krystal's face fell, but she quickly rallied. "Wonderful. I'll let the principal know."

"Fantastic," Eva repeated and smiled widely.

Kill them with kindness. It had been her motto the past ten years. It was a viable alternative to killing women like Krystal Diamond. But Eva had left that part of her behind when she fled Sicily. That way of life felt like a vague memory—something another person had experienced, somebody she'd read about in a book. So, Krystal Diamond was safe. For now.

The woman had apparently kept her maiden name, which was about the only thing Eva approved of about the pretentious PTA head. But what kind of name was Krystal Diamond, anyway? Jesus. It had to be a stripper name. Or maybe a porn star name.

Eva shifted in her uncomfortable plastic chair. She wasn't overweight, and was, in fact, very fit from a daily home workout modeled after the Navy SEAL team's training. But she was Italian and did have curves—especially on her backside. Her backside simply wouldn't fit into this tiny, orange plastic chair made for a fifth grader.

A FEW SEATS down Nikos shifted uncomfortably, as well. He caught her eye and smiled. She smiled back.

Luckily, Krystal Diamond had missed it all. Smiling was forbidden unless the smile was directed her way. But Krystal was at the front of the room, distracted with her head down, going through a thick file folder. Yeah, definitely a fake name. Like her boobs. No way they were the real deal. No. Way. No one with boobs that big could have a butt small enough to fit neatly into the little orange plastic chair, could they? No self-respecting Malibu trophy wife would go that big, even when your husband was the top plastic surgeon to the stars. Eva frowned. Maybe that was it—Dr. Andrew Wyatt used his wife as a model for his porn star clientele. Eva could just imagine him waving his skinny little arms and saying, "Allow me to show you my work first hand. Krystal, darling? Please show these women your tits."

Eva snuffled back a laugh.

Nikos shot her a glance of alarm but then winked. He was her age and attractive. She knew it was his Greek heritage that appealed to her. Even though she'd married a hot American man with blonde hair and blue eyes, she couldn't deny that men from her part of the world had an undeniable, earthy sexiness about them.

That diversity was one reason she'd enrolled Lorenzo and Alessandra in this elite school. Though she had to put up with people like Krystal, the student population ran the gamut from Somali-Americans to Japanese-Americans. She didn't want her children to feel like misfits in Beverly Hills schools. But she had to admit, the Rembrandt Academy still didn't exactly provide a realistic slice of American life—every family with a kid in the school was filthy rich.

Speaking of that, why did they even need to do fundraisers, anyway?

Krystal droned on at the front of the classroom, organizing committees and assigning tasks to the thirty parent volunteers crowding the room.

In a way, Eva admired Krystal's leadership skills. And whatever her faults, Eva could not deny that Krystal's son, Yates, was possibly the sweetest child on the planet.

Poor thing couldn't help who his mother was. And he couldn't help his unfortunate name. Who named a baby Yates? Yates Wyatt sounded like a poet wearing a dinner jacket while riding a donkey in the old west. But the kid was a sweetie. His mother wanted him to be a doctor like his father, but he claimed he wanted to be an opera singer. The kid wasn't even out of elementary school, and his parents were already planning out every second of every year until he was thirty!

Alessandra had befriended Yates in the first grade until Krystal had put the kibosh on their playdates. Every time Eva had reached out to her about it, Krystal made some excuse. She usually claimed Yates was busy with Little Mozart or Chinese lessons or some other lame excuse. But every time Alessandra asked him about it the next day, the poor kid said he'd gone straight home and stared at the iPad all evening while his mother locked herself in her office.

Alessandra and Yates resorted to secretly hanging out at school during lunch hour.

Krystal had her back turned, doing something with the iBoard, so Eva snuck a glance at the time on her phone. Crap. Twenty more long minutes. She'd planned to swing by Delmonico's and pick up a platter of sashimi and a sesame kale salad for dinner. She also wanted to grab a ham and cheese brioche for Matthew's breakfast. He'd texted that his flight had been bumped up, so he'd have to head straight to the airport in the early hours the next morning.

He'd promised that when he returned, he'd take an entire week off for a staycation and they could unwind and make love every day while the kids were at school.

She could hardly wait. She sighed and stretched languidly.

Krystal heard the sigh and shot her a sharp look.

"Mrs. White, did you have a question?"

She smiled. "No. But thanks for asking."

Krystal turned her attention toward another victim. Heidi, the mother of one of Alessandra's good friends.

Nikos grinned at her again. He held up his phone, keeping it below the level of the table. He was playing a video game. He mimicked a yawn and then scraped back his chair. All heads turned his way. He stood and held his phone up in the air. "Sorry. I just got a text. Emergency at the office."

And with that he was gone.

Eva stared at his retreating back with undisguised jealousy. What the hell? Is that all it took? A fake emergency? He'd been playing a video game.

"As I was saying..." Krystal said in the front of the room, clearly annoyed.

For a split-second Eva felt sorry for her. After all, the woman's entire life revolved around the annual school carnival. As soon as one year's event was over, Krystal would send out emails about what they would do the following year. Planning for the event began six months ahead of time.

But then any pity dissipated. Krystal had been downright mean to Eva since the first day of kindergarten orientation four years ago.

And yet, today, here she was volunteering under Krystal's tutelage.

The things she did for her children... Lorenzo had begged her to volunteer, saying if she didn't she'd be the only mother not on the committee.

Reluctantly, she'd agreed.

Someday, when they were older, she'd explain to Lorenzo and Alessandra the sacrifice she'd made kowtowing to such a controlling witch, but for now she'd do whatever it took to make sure she and her family blended in.

Her phone vibrated. Eva looked down.

The picture that appeared on her phone took her breath away. She shot up out of her seat. Her world spun, and her legs grew weak and unsteady. She stumbled, clutching at the table to keep herself from collapsing. Her phone fell to the floor. It landed face up. A photo of a man's severed head filled the screen.

She couldn't get air into her lungs. Her vision closed in. Her legs had grown useless. She slumped back down into her chair and felt a hand on her forearm. It was Heidi's.

"Are you okay?"

The words ignited Eva into action. She scrambled to her feet, grabbed her bag and phone, and began to run, calling "Thank you," over her shoulder to a bewildered Heidi.

She'd barely made it out the door, her three-inch designer heels clacking on the pavement, when someone grabbed her arm and yanked her back.

"Excuse me!" She recognized the high-pitched squeak. Krystal.

"You did not ask to be excused from the meeting."

"Back off, Krystal."

Eva wrenched her arm free so forcibly, a few of Krystal's fake nails went flying. Krystal spluttered in rage, but Eva was already across the parking lot.

She was almost to her vehicle when the driver of a silver Porsche slammed on the brakes, skidding to a halt inches away from her thighs. She kept running, barely registering the woman's concerned face hanging out the window asking if she was okay.

In her Mercedes SUV, Eva's hands trembled so violently it took her three tries to get the key in the ignition. With her foot pressed to the gas, she fumbled under her seat and unsnapped a small case. She threw it on the passenger seat. As she squealed out of the parking lot, she barely noticed the other cars darting out of her way.

With the salty Pacific breeze whipping her hair, Eva raced down the highway, passing slower cars. She pushed back thoughts of her family. It was dangerous to allow herself to get caught up in sentimentality. It would weaken her. She had to reach deep down and draw from her dark past if her family was going to survive.

Her darkest memories rose to the surface. A moonlit Sicilian night full of bloodshed:

Walls splattered with red arterial spray; pools of coagulated blood turned black; clothing stiff with dried blood; a hand with ruby red fingernails placing the queen of spades card on a motionless chest; a head held by the hair with blood dripping onto the ground out of the jagged flesh that had once connected the neck to the body...

The mutilated body of her Sicilian lover and fiancée sprawled under a white sheet.

It all came back, blotting out the golden Southern California sunshine pouring through her driver's side window.

2

Sicily

The rolling hills of Sicily—so green and lush—rendered a stark contrast to the view of white-capped Mt. Etna soaring above the horizon. Like the majestic volcano, in Sicily, beauty often concealed the darker ways of the world.

The idyllic and scenic Italian island, nestled just off the toe of Italy's boot, was home to some of the most ferocious and coldblooded killers on the planet.

At first, none of this touched Eva. She led a carefree life when she was young. But then she was recruited into the family's business and found she thrived on the thrill of covert missions and delivering secret packages in the dead of night. It took a while for her to realize just what business her family was in—the Mafia.

But it didn't take long for her to adapt.

As a teenager, when her father was sent to prison, she was the one tapped to deliver the important messages—the pizzini—that allowed him to rule from behind bars.

It was standard practice in the Cosa Nostra—the Sicilian Mafia. Because only females could visit Mafiosi in prison, they became messengers. Most of the time, the handwritten messages were delivered on tiny scraps of paper that were then conveyed to the prisoner in code. Other times the women or children who could have physical contact with the prisoner could pass on the pizzini themselves.

Prison officials were none the wiser. It ended up being yet another of the millions of times in history that women were underestimated. After serving as her father's courier for so many years, delivering important pizzini, Eva had proven herself.

Her two half-brothers—Luca and Stefano—resented her for it. But they'd never liked her anyway. They thought they should succeed their Mafioso father—that they should be the ones he turned to and trusted. But her father knew that they were more like their backstabbing mother. They were greedy and immoral and disloyal to a fault.

That's why when Eva turned seventeen, and her father was still in prison, he handed over the reins to her, ordering her to maintain his one unbreakable rule: no matter what the other mob families did, their family would never, ever, participate in the sex trade.

Eva solemnly agreed.

Her half-brothers, consumed by jealousy and greed, immediately made plans to get rid of Eva, believing that without her around, they would take over the family business.

But Eva quickly rose to power in the Mafia world, gaining respect and protection from the other mob bosses. It began at the first mob boss gathering she attended in her father's stead.

While the dons sat around drinking and eating and plotting how to kill a dangerous enemy, they ignored Eva completely. After all, she was only a woman.

They dismissed her and refused to take her seriously. Eva watched as the men grew drunker and meaner and then slipped out when nobody was paying attention.

She returned to the gathering holding the bloody head of the enemy the dons had been plotting to kill. At that moment, she rose above just a "fill-in" for her father and was soon made a woman of honor—a donna d' onore.

As far as Eva knew it was the first time a woman had been initiated into the Sicilian Mafia—Cosa Nostra. Her cominato—initiation—

involved her swearing an oath that she would remain a Mafiosa until her death. During the rite, her father's elderly uncle drew blood from her finger and smeared it on a wooden icon of St. Agatha—the patron saint of rape victims, wet nurses, and those afflicted with breast cancer. The icon was then lit on fire and passed around while Eva chanted that she would burn like the icon if she ever betrayed Cosa Nostra.

Other women had taken over the family business for their husbands and been both feared and respected by the other mob bosses, but her father told her she was the first woman ever initiated into the Costa Nostra. As a result, she became a legend to the children of Sicily. Little girls dressed all in black like Eva and played with sticks pretending they were swords.

For two years, Eva owned the world. At least her small world on the island of Sicily.

She stole from the rich and gave to the poor.

The people loved her. They called her "Eva the Saint" or "The Godmother."

She grew into a ruthless assassin but only killed those who deserved to rot in hell. Her calling card—left on all her victims—was the queen of spades. A card that signaled death in Sicily.

Soon, all her other nicknames were shed, and she was known throughout Italy as the Queen of Spades.

But she was betrayed. Her brothers cut a deal with the other mobsters to participate in the sex trade. When Eva protested, they made her pay. And dearly.

They arranged for their own father to be assassinated in prison so he wouldn't stand in their way any longer. Then they ambushed her men. And killed her lover.

Eva had no choice, she had to kill them both.

Luca was in prison, so she went after Stefano first, killing him without an ounce of regret. Before she could go after Luca, the other mob bosses convened to discuss Stefano's murder and decided that she'd gone too far. Killing her own brother, even a half-brother, was punishable by death. Even if he'd been responsible for killing his own father. It was twisted logic and Eva knew it. The mob bosses said she had no proof that her half-brothers had arranged for their father's death. But a woman had witnessed Eva killing Stefano and that could not be disputed.

Not for the first time, Eva regretted being soft in not killing another woman.

The dons put the contract out on her life; it would never be rescinded.

Eva had no choice but to flee to America and go into hiding. After all, her brother Luca was still alive. He'd worshipped Stefano. He would never let the price on her head be forgotten. Never.

She was nineteen when she first stepped foot on American soil.

Over the years, she'd watched from afar in Los Angeles, reading newspaper accounts as his rule grew larger and more powerful. He'd taken over several other families in Italy. He was more powerful than she'd ever been. And yet, for some reason, he seemed to have forgotten about her.

Until now.

For the past ten years, her youth had seemed a distant memory.

But it had finally caught up to her. She would now have to draw on that life, on that training, on that mentality, on those forgotten skills—if she was going to save her family.

3

Los Angeles

It was a lot easier than he thought it would be.

At first, he'd worried he wouldn't have enough time. He was cutting it close. But for a man like him—who spent hours each day visualizing exactly how something would go down, it would happen like clockwork. He was like the Michael Phelps of the crime world.

He'd read about Phelps. How every day for years, Phelps woke up and visualized the perfect race, then did the same thing when he fell asleep at night. The theory was that when you imagined something in your mind enough, your brain couldn't distinguish between what was real and what you were imagining. As a result, when you visualized it, your brain thought your body was actually doing it.

He loved that.

But just in case, along with his two hours of daily visualization, he'd also put in the work. He'd researched the hell out of every aspect of his plan. Every tiny, minute detail was planned to the second. He would not fail. He'd waited much too long to exact his revenge.

So, of course, when the time had come, all the pieces fell perfectly into place.

It could not have gone better.

Now that the plan was underway, there were a few more wheels to set in motion before he could return home. And when he did, he would be a hero.

He could not wait.

4

LOS ANGELES

Eva was on autopilot. Her focus was on navigating the clogged highway in front of her as quickly and efficiently as she could. Each time Matthew's phone went to voicemail, she hit redial. Over. And over. And over.

The sunset seemed surreal. How could the sky be so full of brilliant sherbet-colored hues—tangerine, pink grapefruit, blood orange —when her life was shattering into a million pieces?

Her eyes were trained on the road ahead of her as she laid on her horn and blew past slower cars on the two-lane highway. Again and again she dialed her husband's cell phone. Each time it went straight to voicemail.

In her mind's eye, she plotted her next steps. Over the years, she'd always had an escape plan in place for the family. Now, it was just a matter of pulling the trigger: Once she got home, she'd gather her family and her bug out bag and drive to San Francisco. They'd catch the next flight to Montreal with the fake passports identifying them as the Smith family from San Jose.

From there, she'd switch passports to the ones showing they were Canadians with the surname Michaud who were going to visit Costa Rica.

Once they arrived in Costa Rica, Eva would arrange for them to start a new life. The kids could grow up learning to surf. Matthew could pursue his love of writing and finish that novel he always spoke about.... It would work. It wouldn't be easy explaining everything to her husband and kids, but that was how it would have to be.

She just needed to get to them in time...

She dialed Matthew's cell phone again. It went to voicemail.

5

The Mercedes skidded to a halt outside her home. She didn't bother taking the key out of the ignition or closing her door. She leaped out of the car and raced toward the house, her Ruger LC9 leading the way in her outstretched arms. Her heart thudded at the sight of the open front door.

As she slipped inside, she kept her arms extended with both hands wrapped around the gun, holding it steady. She stepped out of her heels and padded silently into the foyer. A strange dripping echoed in a whirling vortex of distorted sound. Her entire body shook uncontrollably; the gun wobbled before her.

She found Matthew just beyond the foyer. He lay on the polished marble floor, his head twisted unnaturally at an odd angle. His keys were in his hand, his chest torn open from a deadly spray of bullets. His dead eyes stared upward.

The only outward indication that Eva had just seen her dead husband's body was a sharp intake of breath and a long, slow blink and swallow. There was nothing she could do for him. She stepped over his corpse, her eyes darting from doorway to doorway as she made her way to the great room, where she could already see Alessandra's body.

The back of her daughter's golden head—her hair now dark and matted and thick with clotted blood—rose above the back of the couch. At nearly the same time, she registered Lorenzo's crumpled body in the corner near the TV. His chest was blown wide open; his insides spilled out. At his side, one hand still gripped a massive candlestick.

He'd tried to save his sister.

Eva dropped the gun. It landed oddly and discharged into an end table. She didn't even flinch.

Instead, she sank onto the couch and curled herself around Alessandra's body, cradling her daughter's still form. But her eyes were glued on Lorenzo. She reached an arm out to him. "Come here, baby. Come to mama."

When he didn't move, she reluctantly let go of Alessandra and crawled over to him on her hands and knees. She lifted his limp body, dragged him to the couch, and propped him up next to Alessandra. Then she crawled onto the couch and wrapped her arms around both of her children. Her eyes were wide, staring at nothing, but her body rocked as she sang their favorite Italian lullaby.

6

Los Angeles

The warmth of the morning sunlight flooding the east facing bank of windows woke her.

At first, she thought someone was tugging on her hair. When she pulled away, her hair made a crackling sound, and she realized with horror that it had been adhered by blood to her dead daughter's face.

That's when she gave in to the weeping. The howling. The keening. The wailing. The unearthly moaning. She slipped into a semi catatonic state, caught up in memories.

SHE WAS SITTING on the Santa Monica beach at sunset, tears streaming down her face.

She'd been mourning the death of her only friend in L.A.—a Russian girl named Katrina.

The two women had met at the strip club where they worked. Neither were strippers, though. They were waitresses and required to wear skimpy outfits, but nobody was permitted to touch them. The club was for high rollers, and they both made enough money to drink fine bottles of champagne in Katrina's Santa Monica apartment at night.

Once, when Katrina was drunk, she confessed that she was a world-class hacker and that she was in hiding from the government. Eva confessed that she was also in hiding—from the Sicilian Mafia. From that moment on, the two women shared a unique bond.

Katrina spent the next year teaching Eva everything she knew about hacking. Then one night she didn't show up for work. Eva let herself into the Malibu apartment and found Katrina's body. Police said she'd overdosed on heroin. But Eva knew better. The Russians had found her friend.

Blinded by her tears, Eva had stumbled to the beach. She sat there as the sun set, wondering if everyone she loved would be taken away from her. She'd lost Giacomo. Tomas. Her father. Now her only friend. It was too much.

A group of young men playing volleyball nearby packed up and were on their way to the parking lot when one of them stopped.

He asked if he could sit with her. She didn't answer. He sat beside her, and they both stared straight ahead at the sunset.

"It's stunning, isn't it?" he asked without looking at her.

She sniffled. She didn't want to talk to some guy who'd just plopped down on the sand beside her like he owned the damn beach or something. The setting sun caught the blonde hairs on his muscular legs, making them appear to be strands of fine, spun gold.

"When I see something like this," he continued, "it makes me so damn grateful to be alive. I can't believe I'm lucky enough to be sitting right here, right now. If you would've told me about this moment five years ago, I would've told you that you were certifiable. I was an addict. By all accounts, I should be dead or in jail right now. But for some reason, something out there —call it God, call it what you will—thought I should live to see another sunset like this one."

She looked over at him, her curiosity getting the best of her. He was so damn sincere. Before he turned his head toward her, she quickly looked away. She could feel him staring.

The wind was whipping her long dark hair around her head so, at

FIRST, he hadn't noticed her tear-streaked face. When he did, he reached for her hand. He held it silently until the sun dipped below the horizon and the moon and stars came out. She told him she'd lost her entire family to violence in Sicily and was in hiding, but that it was too painful to talk about. He never questioned her or pushed her to reveal more.

That night they made love. A month later they were married.

Eva had been in America only two months when she became a U.S. citizen. Matthew still had contacts from his former life. She was given a new identity when she became his wife.

Eva loved him. But she kept her heart guarded, afraid to love too much. And then they had children. The love she felt for them was indescribable—something she never dreamed possible. The floodgates of her emotions spilled open, and she found herself crying at odd moments of the day, overcome with love for her children and her husband and her life in America. Like Matthew that first day on the beach, she often found herself in awe of the life so rich in love she now led.

Now, sitting on the couch hugging the bodies of her dead children, Eva opened her eyes. Weak from grief and lack of food, she rose unsteadily from the couch.

Eyes dry, she walked over to the other sprawling white leather couch and removed the furry blankets her family used to cuddle up during Friday Family Movie Night. She took the first one and put it over Matthew's body in the hall.

She knelt and kissed his mouth. His lips were icy cold. She put her head down, her hair falling over his face, and whispered in his ear: "You are my angel. You saved me. I will remain yours forever."

Then she returned to the great room, grabbed the other two blankets, and scooped up her gun.

She gently rearranged her children's bodies so they were lying on separate ends of the couch, their heads propped up on the armrests. She paused, staring at them one last time before she bowed and tenderly kissed each one's cheek. As she did, she whispered in their ears, a message of a mother's unending love. She placed the blankets over her children, covering their faces, and left the room, heading to the second story.

7

Los Angeles

Designing a master bedroom and bath had been a dream come true for her. Matthew had given her carte blanche to work with the architect to create it.

At the time, she'd told Matthew she wanted to surprise him with the finished product, so it was all very hush-hush.

In reality, it was because she needed a safe room. A bug-out room. She would never sleep soundly without knowing it existed. But telling Matthew about it meant telling him why she needed it. That could never happen.

To pay off the architect to keep her secret, she'd sold a diamond pendant that Matthew had bought her. She'd also been socking away money and investing it, building a small, secret fortune behind Matthew's back. She siphoned off a little each month out of their bottomless bank account and invested it. Within a year, the first twenty-five grand she'd "borrowed" had quadrupled.

Learning investment strategy at the hands of a master back in Sicily had paid off.

Before she invested her profits, she returned the borrowed twenty-five thousand dollars into their joint account even though Matthew had told her dozens of times she should spend as much of it as she wanted. He'd joked that if she wanted to, she could light a bonfire with cash...as long as it made her happy.

She invested seventy-five thousand in high-risk stocks. Once she hit ten million in profits, she put it in an offshore account under a corporate name. Everything was done under a corporate name. There was no trace of Eva Lucia Santella from Sicily. She'd made sure of that. And there was barely any paper trail for Evangeline White—the name she'd taken upon marrying Matthew. When she told him she'd lost all her official documents when fleeing Italy, he helped her obtain a social security number and citizenship.

But even with a new identity, she still kept under the radar. It was why, for example, she'd never volunteered to chaperone a field trip. They ran full background checks on parents who did. She couldn't afford to risk it. She probably should've changed her first name entirely, but she never thought they'd search for an Evangeline. Only an Eva. And if they had already narrowed their search down to Evangeline White, it was all over anyway.

Deceiving him felt awful, but if she was going to continue her life as Mrs. Matthew White, she needed that safe room and all it contained. She'd had the construction done when Matthew and the kids were in Portland for two weeks visiting his parents.

They were gone now too. His mother died from a stroke, and his father had a heart attack twenty-four hours later. The local newspaper had even written about their deaths, saying her father-in-law had died of a broken heart.

Eva wondered if she could have that same blessing. If her heart stopped beating, at least the unbearable pain would go away.

Although she'd discarded her previous life, she knew she had to be prepared in case the past caught up to her. But she hadn't prepared enough. While their home had a state-of-the-art security system, Matthew never understood how vital it was. If she'd only had the courage to confess everything to him, instead of trying to live a normal life and blend in... She'd let her defenses slip and had paid the ultimate price: the lives of everyone she loved.

She would never forgive herself.

Her secrets had cost her family their lives. And destroyed hers.

She stumbled through the master bedroom, past the king-sized feather bed and the bank of windows overlooking the deck and Pacific Ocean, past the man cave she'd designed for Matthew that was disguised as a walk-in closet but contained a small gym, sauna, and luxurious bathroom.

Inside her walk-in closet, behind a row of designer dresses was a small, hidden button. She pressed it and the entire wall slid open.

Pushing aside the silk, wool, and cashmere garments, she stepped inside.

The room looked the same as it had when she'd last checked on it six months ago when Matthew and the kids had gone to visit his sisters.

Eva had successfully avoided the trips to Portland their entire marriage.

At her wedding, she'd overheard the four sisters talking. They hated her.

They wanted him to get back together with his ex-girlfriend—a woman exactly like them who still lived in the same Portland neighborhood and ran in the same social circles they did. She'd been their best friend for life. There was no competing with that.

Eva had paused breathlessly outside the door at the church and listened to them rip her apart. From her olive skin to the way she wore low-cut tops, high heels, and tight pants. They said she dressed like a hooker and that she flirted with their husbands.

Eva nearly gasped at that. Like she would ever give those pigs the time of day. They leered at her behind their wives' backs, and one had even tried to kiss her one night after a barbecue. She'd grabbed his forearm, wrenched it behind his back, and told him if he ever tried that again, she'd make sure his luck ran out with his beautiful wife.

She'd not only rejected his advances, but she'd also defended her future sister-in-law.

And yet, on her wedding day, they were talking bad about her.

They made fun of her accent. They called her a Goomba. A Real Housewives of New Jersey wannabe. It went on until someone else opened the door at the end of the hall, and Eva fled into a nearby room, closing the door and locking it behind her. She slumped against the door, fighting back tears that quickly turned to anger.

A half hour later, she squared her shoulders and walked down the aisle with her chin held high. She was grateful she'd seen the sisters-in-law's true colors before she'd given her heart to them any further. From then on, she would always be exceedingly polite but aloof. She'd never let them into her world. Not one inch.

And oddly enough, Matthew never argued with her decision to skip the annual trips to Portland. Which told her more than he realized. He'd known all along that his sisters hated her. Her bowing out gave him the freedom to maintain those relationships. She didn't begrudge him that. She didn't expect him to draw a line in the sand. She was Italian after all. She understood loyalty.

But more than that, she would never deprive her children of that big family experience—being doted on by aunts and uncles and forging close friendships with cousins. Because despite their dislike of her, Matthew's family did dote on their children. And that almost made up for it all.

Lost in memories of her wedding as she stood numb with grief in her safe room, Eva realized she'd have to call her sisters-in-law and tell them. She closed her eyes. Later.

Her safe room was well lit by a massive skylight that matched the one over the bed that had given her so many pleasurable nights staring up at the moon and stars—just like when she'd been a little girl in Sicily and fallen asleep on a grassy hill stargazing.

A desk held a titanium laptop. One wall was essentially a large cabinet.

Eva stood dazed in the middle of the room, taking it all in, mentally cataloguing what was inside each cubby, drawer, cabinet, and closet.

One drawer contained burner phones. A large door opened to display her arsenal. Another cupboard held a duffel bag full of cash,

and there was more in a safety deposit box at her bank. A locker sized cabinet held her clothes. Another closet held her bug-out bag.

Although she knew she needed to hurry, she was paralyzed. Her legs wouldn't move. Her arms stayed stuck to her side and her feet glued to the ground. Only her eyes darted from place to place.

Daggers. Swords. Guns. Bug-out backpack. Laptop. Cell phones. Change of clothes. Boots.

Her eyes traveled down to her feet. She was covered in blood. It triggered something within her, and slowly, she stripped. Standing in the same spot, she peeled the blood-crusted clothes from her body and let them drop at her feet. The blinking green cursor on the black screen of her laptop was hypnotizing. With the press of a button she'd be able to watch the surveillance footage of everything that had happened in her home over the past twenty-four hours. She shook her head as if to clear it.

She stepped out of the clothes puddled at her feet and opened the cabinet with the large bug-out backpack inside. It contained several changes of clothing and a first aid kit, but she needed to add the other items. First, she opened the gun cabinet. She picked out a second handgun —a Sig Sauer P238. Guns were not her weapon of choice, but she also knew better than to bring a knife to a gunfight. She stuck the Sig Sauer and her Ruger in their special slots inside the backpack. Then she filled a large duffel bag with ammunition.

She opened the cabinet where she kept her most treasured weapons—the knives, daggers, and swords she'd grown to love when studying Gladiatura Moderna in Sicily. She picked out two of each and placed the knives and daggers in a special padded case and also tucked that into the bugout bag. The swords she slipped into special padded cases that were attached to the bug-out bag.

She was done within moments. She'd trained and timed herself. She glanced at the clock but knew there was no hurry.

They weren't coming after her. If they'd wanted her dead, they would've waited and killed her when she walked in. No. Her punishment was living with the slaughter of her family. To Luca, her suffering was more important than the price on her head.

Still nude, she sat down at the laptop and logged off, then stuck it into its special compartment in the backpack. From a drawer, she pulled out a tightly bundled package containing $10,000 in cash. She grabbed four burner cell phones and tucked them and the cash in another pocket of the pack before she set it and the duffel bag just outside the doorway.

She opened the closet door and pulled some clothes off a hanger: tight black pants, a black long-sleeve T-shirt, and a black jacket.

Clutching the clothes, she scooped up a pair of knee-high black boots and dipped her head back through the clothes lining the doorway to her secret room.

She shut the door behind her and rearranged the rack of clothing, so it hid the entrance to the secret room. It wasn't really necessary. Even with the clothes pushed aside, it looked like a blank wall behind them. But she wanted to delay discovery of the room for as long as possible.

She stepped into her massive shower and cleaned herself as quickly as she could, scrubbing with soap and letting the water beat down on her head until the red swirling down the drain turned clear.

8

Los Angeles

When she stepped off the bus at Union Station, she was no longer Evangeline White. Nor was she Eva Lucia Santella. She was the Queen of Spades.

Dressed all in black with her blonde hair tucked underneath a black knit stocking cap, Eva pulled back her shoulders and stepped back into her decade-old persona.

She wasn't a rich Malibu housewife.

She was a mob boss. One of the first women in Italy to be made a donna d' onore.

One of the first women to be the head of a Mafia family.

Not only was she one of the first—she was the best.

She was a legend.

For ten years, there'd been a price on her head. The Mafia dons said it was because she'd killed her brother, but she knew the truth. They didn't want a woman leading a Mafia family—especially one who refused to participate in the sex trade.

When the hit on her came out from the mob bosses across Italy, she turned to her last hope, a childhood friend who had become a priest. Tomas had risked everything and ultimately gave his life to help her to escape to America.

As her plane flew over her homeland, she received a text photo of Tomas's dead body. Her grief and anguish had nearly been the death of her. She'd wanted to hijack the plane, turn it around, and avenge Tomas even if it cost her own life.

In her grief, she turned toward a flask of wine Tomas had given her, telling her to raise it in a toast when she passed over Sicily. She'd already downed the wine, and now she realized she'd been drugged. She struggled to stand and go confront the pilots, but instead sank into her seat and then into oblivion.

When she woke, near America, she realized what Tomas had done. He'd known his help would cost his own life. He'd spiked the wine to make sure she got to America.

Knowing that Tomas felt it was worth his own life for her to escape, gave her the strength to start a new life in America.

But now all bets were off.

The same people who'd murdered her lover, Giacomo, and her oldest friend, Tomas, had now massacred her entire family. Although she had no proof, she was certain Luca was behind it all. She would not rest until he'd paid with his own life.

Fired up with bloodthirst, Eva stood before the woman at the front desk of the Little Tokyo motel and thrust a wad of one-hundred-dollar bills at her. She'd never paid attention to what a hotel room cost before. Matthew had always taken care of that sort of thing.

Eva had scoped out this motel a few years ago. It was nearly buried, practically invisible within the windowless walls of a rundown mall in Little Tokyo.

The woman at the front desk didn't speak English but plucked a one hundred-dollar bill out of the wad Eva shoved at her and held up two wrinkly, age-spotted fingers. Two nights. Which probably meant that Eva had paid for about a week, but that was fine.

Two nights was all Eva needed to get the ball rolling in her new life.

The room itself smelled like mold and urine, but Eva didn't care.

After she locked the door behind her, she took out her laptop and set it up on the small dresser, pulling the bed close enough to sit on. But before she logged on, she took a deep breath and flicked on the TV.

The volume was overly loud, but she remained frozen, listening, and staring.

The well-coiffed TV reporter with the orange bodycon dress stood in front of the iron gate leading to Eva's driveway and home. How had she gotten there that quickly? Eva had taken a bus to Little Tokyo and transferred twice, but she still didn't understand. How did anyone even know about the crime yet? She swallowed the word down. Crime. Massacre. Slaughter.

She shook it away. She didn't have time to grieve. Not until she had avenged her family's murders.

The screen cut to an aerial shot. A news helicopter's camera footage showed her home surrounded by emergency vehicles. Three ambulances. A firetruck. Five squad cars. All with the lights off. There was no hurry.

A blue sedan pulled into view. A man with silver-streaked dark hair, aviator sunglasses, and a black blazer stepped out of the driver's seat, and the uniformed officers at the front door parted to let him in.

A detective.

Mesmerized by what she was watching, Eva was jolted when the screen cut back to the newsroom. A TV anchor with cheekbones that could cut glass was talking earnestly about the scene.

"Investigators aren't releasing specifics about the crime scene but said that multiple bodies were found inside the home. They also are asking for information on this woman."

Eva gasped when her picture appeared on the screen. It was a photograph taken by Matthew when they were on their honeymoon in Cabo San Lucas. She had been on the beach laughing, and the wind had blown her hair partially in her face. It was the only photograph she'd allowed taken of her since she came to America. Matthew had not questioned her aversion to cameras, but he'd begged to take this one. She'd been so in love and in such a good mood that day, she'd relented. He'd promised to never post it online.

She'd allowed him to print it as an 8x10, and he'd put it in a Tiffany frame and kept it on his dresser in their bedroom. The frame had cost a small fortune.

At the time, Eva wasn't used to her TV producer husband's extravagant spending and deep pockets. As she stood staring at her own picture on the TV screen, she was jolted back to the present by something the reporter said.

"Investigators have just released some new information. They say the woman in the photo lived here with her family. And now she is missing."

"Belinda," said the man in the newsroom. "Are they saying she is a victim, say of a kidnapping?"

"They aren't saying."

"Is she a suspect?"

"Okay, well thank you, Belinda. Folks, we'll remain out on the scene until we find out more about this horrific situation. Stay tuned."

The screen flickered to a commercial for an air freshener. Eva stayed standing, staring, the remote control at her feet.

A suspect.

Well, that crap would be dispelled as soon as investigators reviewed the surveillance footage.

As the broadcast ended, Eva turned away from the screen and caught a glimpse of herself in the full-length mirror. There was no shortage of mirrors in the room. There was even one on the ceiling that was hazy and black from the silver backing oxidizing over decades.

Her appearance was a far cry from her soccer mom getup. There were no pressed white Capri pants with kitten heels and a pink cashmere sweater.

Dressed all in black with her blonde-streaked hair tucked under the cap, Eva knew her disguise wouldn't be enough. The monthly trips to the salon to make her black hair a light brown with blonde streaks had made her fit in.

But it was time to return to her roots.

She pulled out two boxes of hair dye from the bottom of her bugout bag. They were crumpled and several years old, but she assumed they would still do the trick. She laid them out on the bed. Redhead? Black?

She picked up the box of black dye. She'd gone blonde simply to disguise herself from those in Sicily who'd known her with black hair.

That was no longer necessary.

Now she had to disguise herself from police who would be asking too many questions. She needed to stay under the radar until she avenged her family's deaths.

And she had to hurry. Once police viewed the surveillance video, they'd be looking for the killer. She had to beat them to it. She wondered whether Luca had come to America himself or if he sent someone else to do his dirty work. Either way she would take her revenge. Kill the murderer and then Luca. If he was the killer, it would be that much easier.

The governor had recently rescinded the death penalty in California. Life in prison was too good for the monster who'd taken her family away from her. Even execution at the hands of the state was too easy a way to die.

She needed to exact her own form of revenge.

Then, with her enemy's blood on her hands, she'd be happy to talk to the authorities. She'd be relieved to turn herself in. Because at that point, she'd have nothing left to live for. She'd sworn an oath of vendetta. Exacting it would be her last act.

9

Eva woke early. Before dawn. The night before, she'd lain on top of the motel's sheets in her underwear and a large T-shirt, staring at the ceiling until she'd realized sleep was impossible.

Only then had she rummaged into her first aid kit and taken two sleeping pills.

As a result, she'd had soul-wrenching, gutting nightmares. She tossed and turned amid images of blood and her family's bodies come to life blaming her for their deaths.

When she woke, her hair was soaked with sweat and tears.

Within an hour, she was blow drying her new black hair. The sink was filled with four inches of blonde hair she'd cut off with scissors from the first aid kit. She carefully bagged up the hair and stuck it deep in her bag. Hair had DNA.

She had only one goal—to stay underground until her vendetta was fulfilled.

Now, lying on the motel room bed in the dark, she quickly worked through her plans and what she had to do next.

She'd taken the first steps of her escape plan years ago. While Matthew and the kids were in Portland, she took three trips. She flew to New Mexico,

Nevada, and Wyoming and set herself up as a limited liability company. In those three states, corporations were not required to record the name of their owners.

Then she opened bank accounts and credit cards through her LLCs using some of the money from her offshore account. She wanted the accounts and cards just in case, but mostly she planned to use the accounts to withdraw cash or purchase prepaid debit cards.

She'd also learned how to program her four burner phones with throw-away phone numbers. She could create one right before she made a call and then delete it after.

Now, she planned to buy a house outright in Los Angeles using a cashier's check and the LLC's identity. She needed a secure home base while she hunted.

Because, make no mistake, she was hunting. And she wouldn't rest until she had killed.

As soon as it grew light, she'd contact a luxury real estate agent and explain her situation. A cash deal. Property bought through a corporation. No face-to-face meetings. Photos, video, and blueprints of the property would be enough.

With her new black hair and wardrobe—along with ubiquitous, massive black sunglasses to thwart facial-recognition software—she'd hopefully be unrecognizable as the blonde-streaked Malibu housewife who'd dressed in designer clothes and carried a Louis Vuitton bag.

Her laptop wasn't a problem. The IP address was never connected to her Malibu home. She'd long ago created a VPN, a virtual private network, that redirected her internet traffic, bouncing her supposed location to destinations around the world.

Her Mercedes was a thing of the past. She'd use the LLC to buy a "sleeper car"—an innocuous, common car with some under-the-hood get up and go. After she did a little research on her laptop in the Little Tokyo motel, Eva picked out a used, white Subaru Forester on Craig's List.

She'd arrange for the real estate agent to pay for it and then Eva would register it to a small home in Boyle Heights that she'd bought last year for just that purpose. The home was a crumbling three sided structure that was barely standing and was most definitely not habitable. The last time she'd checked, used needles and beer cans littered its dirt floor.

She'd also used that address to set up a post office box under a false name and enlisted a remailing service that took mail, shipped it to another state and then shipped it back to any address she desired.

As she realized all she'd done to prepare for her life in Sicily to catch up to her, Eva hung her head in shame. Her entire life with Matthew had been a lie. He hadn't deserved that. If only she had told him and trusted him, he and their kids might still be alive.

Instead, while she played Malibu housewife and mother, her secretive part-time job was planning for her identity to be revealed. But in her plans, she and her family all went into hiding together. It was not supposed to have happened like this. They were supposed to disappear to Costa Rica or the mountains or to an island somewhere.

Checking her watch, she realized she had at least another hour before she could contact the real estate agent she had in mind. A small icon on the corner of her home screen kept drawing her eye. It was the folder that contained the automatically downloaded surveillance footage from the previous day.

Her heart pounded, and her face felt icy. Trying to ignore the folder, she logged online using a personal hotspot and VPN that couldn't be traced to her seedy motel room. Instead, anyone trying to track it would be bounced around Russia and Bolivia and Greenland, among other places.

It took less than twenty minutes for her to find a house. For five million, most people would consider it a fixer upper. It was outdated with carpet and wood paneling in the bedroom, but she didn't care about any of that. And it was furnished. But what attracted her was the location. Not just that it was in Hollywood Hills, but where it was in the hills.

From the satellite images, she saw the home was perched high on top of its own little hill with a massive iron gate and guard shack. A winding driveway bordered with dense and difficult brush led up from a residential road with only a few other houses on it. The hillside below the house was thick with dense brush. Most people would view it as a terrible fire hazard. Eva saw it as a fortress.

In addition, the house had a small back deck overlooking downtown Los

Angeles. From there, she could see the entirety of the residential road that wound up to the house from Franklin Avenue. That meant she would see any vehicles heading her way from a mile out.

Her mind raced with the modifications she had in mind. Some would be through the real estate agent: a security system installed at the gate with cameras and the ability to open the gate from the house and another state-of-the-art security system for the house and grounds. She figured getting the systems installed immediately and expediting the purchase of the house would cost her a pretty penny, but that didn't matter.

Some modifications she would make on her own: a sensor a mile down the road that would trigger an alarm and cameras to film any vehicle that drove over it.

She decided to do a little research on the neighbors. She dug up everything available online for the seven other people who lived on the small road. Nobody triggered any alarms. They were all upper middle class working families for the most part.

Perfect.

In two days, she would be settled in her new home and ready to hunt.

At nine she called the real estate agent. She put on her voice encryptor headphones with the mic that made her sound like a man.

It took an hour on the phone, but the real estate agent promised the house would be ready in two days. She would mobilize a team and get it all done that day. With the amount of money Eva was offering for the extra services, she could afford to get it done within 48 hours. The real estate agent said it would be tough but she could get it arranged and she'd program a temporary code into the gate so Eva could access the property immediately.

When Eva hung up, she quickly made the wire transfer and, once she saw it was sent, sat back staring at the screen.

She couldn't put it off any longer.

She had to view the surveillance video. She rewound the video until she saw Matthew's Range Rover pull into the driveway.

Eva pressed play, resuming the footage at normal speed.

Matthew stepped out of the car. When Lorenzo and Alessandra clamored out, Eva made a strangled gasping sound. Clutching at the mouse pad she scrambled to hit pause. Something was lodged in her throat. There was no place left for the air. She stared at the image of her children on the screen. She enlarged the picture, 50 percent, 100 percent, 200 percent until the image pixelated and fractured, transforming flesh into small colored squares of pink and beige. She zoomed back out until she could again see their faces and then reached out her hand, her fingers nearly touching the screen where her dead children were frozen in time.

Time passed. She wasn't sure whether it was fifteen seconds or fifteen minutes before she hit play and the video resumed. Her children raced into the house, their faces wide with smiles. Matthew followed, his head down, frowning.

Had he sensed impending doom, or had it just been a bad day at work? In his job as a producer on a sitcom, he sometimes came home exasperated with the unrealistic demands of actors. On those days, Eva always suggested they sit out on their private master bedroom deck and watch the sunset while the children did homework and took their baths.

Eva was about to flick to the cameras showing the inside of the home, the foyer, and great room, but she paused. There was something dark in the corner of the screen.

It was right at the first curve in the driveway leading away from the house. A vehicle.

Painstakingly, she clicked forward one frame at a time. As soon as the vehicle emerged fully into the frame, she stopped the video. She blew up the picture as large as she could while keeping it somewhat clear. The vehicle was a black Mercedes SUV. The same model she drove. The same vehicle that many people in Malibu owned. She couldn't make out the license plate number.

Heart pounding, she started the video again, slowly, frame by frame.

The Mercedes came to a stop right behind Matthew's Range Rover. Eva held her breath as the driver's side door was flung open. The driver moved fast.

For a second, Eva froze. She'd assumed the killer was a man. But this person had long hair hanging down his or her back from underneath a ball cap.

The clothing—baggy pants and an oversize jacket—didn't give any indication of gender. And the person's head was tucked low, the face hidden from the overhead camera. She caught a glimpse from the side of massive dark sunglasses further obscuring the person's features. A chill ran through her. It sure looked like a woman.

It seemed impossible that another woman in Sicily had become an assassin like Eva. But maybe not. After all, Eva had been gone ten years.

Eva watched as the person raced up the steps of her home. She hit pause. The person was carrying an assault rifle. She hit play.

The person barged through the open door. Matthew had not yet closed it.

Eva switched cameras to the one in the foyer, but not before closing her eyes for a second, bracing herself. She opened her eyes. Matthew whirled to face the intruder. His chest instantly darkened, and he crumpled to the ground. The killer stepped over his body and ran toward the great room. Alessandra's head was visible over the couch. Within seconds, the back of her head exploded. Her body slumped forward. Lorenzo...her brave boy, lunged forward with a heavy candlestick in his hand. His chest opened up. His eyes and mouth opened and a hand moved down toward his stomach before he collapsed out of view.

Eva knew she should switch cameras so she could view the scene from the camera in the great room. Her chest and throat were tightening. Her heart was pounding so hard she vaguely wondered if it was what a heart attack felt like.

As she sat in a paralyzed daze, the footage continued to roll. Her eyes glassy, she watched the gunman turn back toward the foyer camera. It wasn't a man.

Under the hat and sunglasses, Eva saw dark lipstick on full lips.

The woman stopped right underneath the camera and yanked off the ball cap. Blonde-streaked hair tumbled out. She pushed the sunglasses up on her head and stared straight at the camera.

Eva gasped and screamed, knocking the laptop over as she jerked to her feet.

The face looking up at her was her own.

10

Los Angeles and Sicily

"It is done."

"You will return home a hero." The man was in Sicily, but it sounded like he was in the same room. Approval and pride filled his voice. "We will make arrangements for you to return home within the month."

"I'd prefer sooner."

"We will make arrangements for you to return within the month." The line disconnected.

11

LOS ANGELES

Right after the woman with her face had looked up at the camera, she'd raised a gun and shot out the camera and then methodically did the same thing to all the other cameras in the house.

Eva had stared at the black screen for a few seconds before turning it off.

She felt hollow and numb inside. Every time thoughts of her family popped into her head, she angrily dismissed them. Not now. Later. Later she would allow herself the luxury of remembering them. She would give herself this gift on her death bed.

She would start at the beginning for each of them. She'd begin with Matthew on the Santa Monica beach and then remember every second with him until she kissed him goodbye the day of his murder. For Lorenzo, she'd start with the second she realized she was pregnant and remember every little detail of him in her life—his birth, his first bite of food, his first smile, giggle, step, day of kindergarten. Every single thing. And then she'd do the same for Alessandra. Start with that day she and Matthew made love secretly, giggling, trying not to wake Lorenzo who was asleep in the bassinet just one wall away. And how as soon as they were done, Matthew had known. "I just got you pregnant."

He'd grinned as he said it.

"Whatever," she'd said and laughed.

"I know it."

She'd made a skeptical face but then her eyes had widened. He'd said the same thing the night Lorenzo was conceived.

"Really?" she'd said. She leaned against his shoulder, closing her eyes. "God, I hope so. I want another baby right now."

"Lorenzo isn't even out of diapers."

"I know. I just love being a mother so much. I never expected to feel this way." I never thought I'd be a mother. "I never expected any of this."

"This?" Matthew said drawing back to see her eyes. "What do you mean?"

She sighed loudly. "All of this. This happiness. This blessing. This life."

He drew her close and kissed the top of her head. "You deserve all this and more, my Eva."

She had smiled, but deep down she knew he was wrong. She didn't deserve a second of it. She was a stone-cold killer who deserved to rot in hell for murder. Or at least that's what most people would say.

Now, in the motel room, she put those memories away for later. There was plenty of time left to rot in hell. In fact, maybe she was already there.

For the rest of the day, Eva searched for information about the crime families in Sicily and Southern Italy. Nothing came up about a female assassin or mob boss. Who was this woman who looked like her? She still couldn't quite wrap her brain around the fact that the woman was her doppelganger.

Was it possible that she had a twin sister who'd been raised by someone else? Might her mother have been pregnant with another child when Luca and Stefano had shipped her off to live with her

SISTER IN ROME? And if so, what were the odds that she'd look just like Eva? And why would her sister commit such a horrific act?

Another thought struck her—what if someone hated her so much that they had plastic surgery to look like her? It was too easy to get caught up in such questions—she needed to keep her eye on the prize. Once she found the woman, she'd get all of the answers before she slit her throat.

The next morning, she woke and fumbled for the TV's remote control.

She flipped through the channels until she found what she was looking for—the news.

Within ten minutes, she was looking at a picture of herself staring back at her from the screen. The blown-up surveillance video picture was blurry and slightly pixelated. But it looked like her.

She turned up the volume.

"Police are asking the public's help to find this woman," the newscaster said. "Anyone who has information on her whereabouts is asked to call the crime tip number."

Eva groped for the burner phone she'd set on the nightstand repeating the tip number in her head. After her phone call to the real estate agent, she'd reprogrammed the phone with another burn number. Keeping her eyes on the TV, she dialed the phone number scrolling across the bottom of the TV screen.

"Police."

"This is Eva White," she said without waiting for the other woman to say more. "I need to talk to the detective handling the White family case."

"Ma'am, I am not able to transfer you. This line is only for taking messages. May I take a message?"

"I said this is Eva White. I need to speak to the detective immediately."

"I'm sorry. I can only take messages."

Eva closed her eyes for a second. Fine. She'd get the detective's attention, and he'd take her next call.

"Then take this message down: I did not kill my family. I'm innocent. And I'm going to prove it."

She hung up. What else could she say? Nothing. She deleted the randomly generated phone number from the burner phone and programmed a new one.

Pushing the sheets off her sticky, wet body, she heaved herself to a sitting position, accidentally sticking her foot right in the puddle of vomit near the bed. She ran a hand through her hair.

She stood and made her way to the bathroom where she gulped several handfuls of water while the shower water got warm.

An hour later, she slipped out of the motel's back door wearing a black stocking cap over her newly black hair. She slung both her bugout and duffel bags over her shoulder and trudged in her knee-high boots toward the bus stop at Union Station, a few blocks away.

Inside the bus terminal, she scanned the bus schedules and saw the bus she needed wasn't for another twenty minutes.

For the first time, her stomach grumbled. She couldn't remember the last time she'd eaten. She knew that she'd need to eat to keep up her strength if she was going to hunt down the woman who murdered her family.

Eva felt the weight of her favorite dagger at her back in its scabbard. She would use that special blade to avenge her family. The dagger had belonged to her lover, Giacomo. She had taken it after Stefano had killed him.

With time to kill, Eva ducked into an old-fashioned style diner inside Union Station. Worried she wouldn't keep any food down, she ordered a bland meal—broiled salmon and plain white rice without any spices, herbs, or sauces.

Sitting at the bar, she glanced at the TV screen, which was blaring some chirpy, cheerful newscaster's voice. She flinched. She wondered if her family's murder had been replaced by the crime du jour yet. She soon had her answer.

Krystal's face appeared larger-than-life on the screen. So close, Eva could see the creases in the thick makeup around her mouth. A petite Latina reporter held a microphone up to Krystal.

"Ms. Diamond, you know Eva White?"

Krystal let out a big puff of air. "Yes."

Eva remembered back to the first time she'd met Krystal Diamond four years ago during kindergarten orientation.

The animosity between them had been immediate.

That day, Matthew had taken the day off to treat Lorenzo to a baseball game. Although Alessandra was a good baby, Eva had arranged for the neighbor's college-age daughter to watch her during the school meeting. But when the young woman called and said she was sick, it was already time for Eva to leave. Not wanting to be late, Eva grabbed Alessandra and a diaper bag and headed toward the school.

When she stepped into the cafeteria, she slid into a spot toward the back in case Alessandra got fussy and she had to step outside. The chairs were filled, and the principal had just stepped behind the podium with the microphone when there was a commotion at the back of the room.

A slim blonde with a massive mane of hair, a pink Chanel suit, beige pumps, and a red Kelly handbag slung on one arm walked in, smiling widely at the audience. Eva noticed everyone was smiling back at this woman. She paused before Eva and said, "So nice of you to make it."

For a second, Eva was taken aback. The blonde wrinkled her nose at baby Alessandra and was gone. She took a seat in the front row that had obviously been saved for her.

The principal proceeded to give the details of the kindergarten orientation. As Eva listened, she thought that the information could have been given on a one-page memo. What a royal waste of time.

A half hour into it, the principal introduced the blonde as Krystal Diamond, the head of the Guidance Facilitators Organization. As Eva listened, she realized the GFO was a fancied-up name for PTA—the parent-teacher association. Growing up in Sicily, the PTA, like so many other things, was a foreign concept to her. But fortunately, her neighbor Sue had spoken about the PTA at her daughter's school.

Sue had said it was a way for parents to volunteer.

But as Eva listened, it seemed that the GFO was more of a way for bored, rich parents to boss other bored, rich parents around.

Krystal was in the middle of talking about the annual fundraiser when Alessandra got fussy and started to cry. Eva didn't want to miss the presentation or disturb the rest of the room, so she lowered the scoop neck of her knit top and began to nurse.

She smiled down at Alessandra as the infant fed. Breastfeeding had been another unexpected joy of motherhood. Nothing was sweeter than seeing Alessandra's lips curve into a smile as she paused from nursing to meet her mother's eyes. It was one of the most natural, loving things Eva had ever done for another person.

Suddenly, Eva realized the room had grown silent.

When she looked back up, she met Krystal Diamond's eyes. She froze mid-sentence and was watching Eva with a glare full of both disdain and disgust.

Heads turned to see what she was staring at.

Faced with dozens of people staring at her, Eva froze. Her goal in her new life was to not bring any undue attention to herself. It was crucial for her survival. Her instinct was to tell them all off and turn around, but she knew she couldn't. Instead, she looked away.

A few of the women smiled at her. Others looked at her with indifference.

The principal saved the day, approaching the podium and taking charge.

"Thank you, Krystal. We can go into more details about the fundraiser later."

Eva gave the principal a grateful smile as heads turned back toward the front.

But from that day on, Krystal had been rude to Eva in her passive aggressive manner.

Now, Eva cringed as she watched Krystal on TV and waited for what she would say.

The reporter held the microphone up to Krystal's heavily made-up face.

"Can you tell viewers what happened the last time you saw Eva White?"

Eva's heart sank.

"She was acting really strange," Krystal said. "First, she stood up in the middle of my meeting—I'm in charge of the annual fundraiser; we raise more than $500,000 a year." She smiled at the camera.

"What do you do with the funds you raise?" the reporter asked. "Is there a charity near and dear to your heart?"

The question threw Krystal for a loop. She blinked several times before answering. "Why, the money goes right back into the school. Of course. For technology. I mean our children today need to have top-notch technology if they are going to compete in this world. Every student at our school is given a state-of-the-art laptop, iPad, smartphone, action camera, video editing software...well, I could go on and on about how wonderful our school is."

"It sounds lovely," the reporter said, but her facial expression didn't match her words. She was clearly exasperated with Krystal. She shifted from leg to leg and then plastered a huge smile on her face before saying, "Back to what we were discussing earlier. What did Ms. White do that was strange?"

"Oh yes, that," Krystal said as if even speaking about Eva was bothersome. "She walked out in the middle of the meeting, and when I went after her for an explanation, she became violent."

"Violent? In what way?" For the first time the reporter looked interested.
"She struck me."
"Hit you? Where?"
"She grabbed my arm. She left a mark. She ripped my fingernails off!"
The reporter blanched.

Krystal plucked her red Kelly handbag off her arm, switched it to the other one, and then pushed up the sleeve of her silk blouse. She held out her bare wrist.

Even though the camera zoomed in, her pinkish flesh looked unblemished.

Eva could barely contain her anger. It was a blatant lie. The woman had grabbed her arm and Eva had yanked away. Eva's arm was the one with the mark, the trail of five scratches from Krystal's long fake nails digging into her flesh, drawing blood.

"Oh my," the reporter said. "She ripped your nails off?" She pointedly looked at Krystal's long, pointy, white-painted nails.

Krystal nodded, eyes wide.

The reporter gave the camera a serious look and said, "And then shortly after that incident in the parking lot of the school, Eva.

White's family was murdered." Krystal pursed her lips and nodded.

The reporter patted Krystal's arm and then put a hand to an earpiece, nodding.

"Stand by. Robert? You say you have another parent on the line who just called and says he also knew Ms. White? Let's go back to the newsroom now."

The footage switched back to the news desk. A big graphic with the black silhouette of a man's head, said, "Man who knew Eva White on the line."

Eva instantly recognized the voice. "My name is Nikos Alexopoulos. I've known Ms. White since our children were in preschool, and I wanted to say that there is no way she would ever have done something so heinous. I think the police are wasting their time looking for her as a suspect. She loved her family. She would never have hurt them."

Eva felt tears prick at her eyes but dismissed them. There was no room for weakness. Not now. Not from here on out.

"Did you see the photo that the police released?" the anchor asked.

There was a long silence.

"Mr. Alexopoulos, did you see the photo? Police say the rest of the footage shows that woman killing her family. It's all documented." "Yes. I did see the photo."

"In your opinion, did the woman in the photo look like Eva White."

Another silence.

"Sir?"

"Yes." The voice sounded painful.

"Thank you for your time, Mr. Alexopoulos." The line was disconnected, and Nikos was dismissed.

The TV switched back to the Latina reporter. "Robert, we were just about to leave the school grounds when Krystal Diamond flagged us down. We'll let her explain."

Eva sat up straighter, leaning across the bar toward the TV, straining to hear every word.

Krystal's oversized head appeared in front of the camera again. The person wielding the camera scooted back a bit. Krystal followed, inching forward until the reporter touched her arm, saying in a low voice, "You're perfect standing right here."

"Ms. Diamond, why don't you tell viewers what happened when you went to your car a few moments ago?"

"My tire was flat!" She said it as if the idea was inconceivable.

"And what else?" the reporter prompted.

Krystal blinked. Deer in headlights. "Didn't you say you found something?" "Yes..." she trailed off, seeming dazed.

The reporter waited. Krystal blinked again.

"Do you want to just hold it up?"

That seemed to prompt Krystal back to life.

"Yes, I found this on my seat. Which I don't understand, because I always lock my Lexus, and there is an alarm, but this was on my seat." She sounded bewildered as she held up a playing card. The queen of spades.

Eva stifled her gasp. She quickly looked around at the other people seated at the bar, but nobody was paying attention—to her or the TV. The bartender, however, cast her an odd look, and she realized she needed to get the hell out of there.

Leaving a twenty-dollar bill on the bar and most of the meal she'd ordered untouched, she scooped up her bags and slipped out the door into the main terminal. She walked quickly as she made her way to the place where her bus was waiting.

As she walked, her chest tightened. The message was crystal clear. No pun intended. The killer was going after that Queen Bee diva next and wanted Eva to know.

Krystal was bait. The killer was baiting her. She knew exactly who Eva was. She was right, her past had caught up with her.

The message was unmistakable.

Eva felt no urge to save the nasty woman, but she knew she would, if only to prevent Krystal's sweet son from going through such a tragedy.

As she stepped on the bus, she felt a sense of urgency swarm through her. She needed to get set up and on the hunt immediately. She'd already wasted too much time. The killer was expecting her, waiting for her. She'd made that clear with the playing card. And one other thing was clear—the clock was ticking.

12

Los Angeles

After the bus let her off on Sunset Boulevard, Eva flagged down a taxi to take her the rest of the way to her house. The neighbors would do a double take if they saw her trudging up the long, steep road carrying her bug-out bag and a duffel. It was conspicuous to say the least.

The taxi driver dumped her at the guardhouse gate.

"Thanks. I'm visiting friends. They'll be home in a minute. I'll just wait here." She was careful to pay the exact amount with a normal tip. She didn't want anything about her to stand out in the taxi driver's mind. It was bad enough that she looked like a homeless vagabond with all her gear.

When the taxi's taillights disappeared around a corner, Eva punched in the gate code she'd given to the real estate agent. Bingo. So far so good. After the gate swung closed behind her, she took note of all the security cameras she'd asked the real estate agent to have installed. They were all in place. Once she made it inside the house, she'd set up her laptop and transfer the remaining funds to the agent.

She hadn't seen any people or vehicles, so she headed up the steep, winding driveway.

The house itself was nondescript. It had no windows on the front side, a feature Eva found very appealing. Instead, the bulk of the front of the stucco house was comprised of a two-car garage and a solid door. When she'd stepped inside the house and locked the door behind her, she let her shoulders sag in relief.

One step down. A million more to go. She was just on the brink of the hunt, still in the planning and preparation stages. But luckily, the killer had given her a map. She knew exactly where to go and what to do. She needed to hurry, though.

She peeked into the attached garage. The car she'd requested was there with a full tank, registration, and keys in the ignition. Perfect. Back inside, she set up her laptop on the granite bar counter and logged in. The first thing she did was pay the real estate agent.

She left a note: "Excellent work. I've transferred the remaining funds."

Then she logged into the new security system for the house and checked the footage going all the way back to installation. Nothing seemed unusual or out of place.

Although she was eager to act, Eva had to sit tight for a few hours. Krystal would be at the school for the rest of the day, working in the school library like she did every Thursday. Eva would wait outside the school until the library closed at five and then follow her home. Just to be safe, though, Eva grabbed her voice encryptor headphones and programmed them to portray a female voice before connecting them to her burner cell phone and dialing the school's main line.

"Is Krystal Diamond there?" she said. "I can't believe it, but my son forgot to turn in his library book today. I reminded him several times."

"Yes. Ms. Diamond is in the library. Would you like me to transfer you?"

"I don't want to disturb her. Just one question, though—do you know how long she'll be there? If I leave now, will I still be able to get it to her in time?" The woman on the other line seemed exasperated by her questions.

"I don't know where you are coming from or how long it will take you, so I can't answer that question. However, I can tell you that Ms. Diamond is scheduled to work in the library until five p.m. today since the library is open late on Thursdays now instead of Mondays."

"Perfect. Thanks. I'll be there before five."

Eva hung up, disabled the generated number, and programmed a new one.

She had several hours before she had to leave for school.

Enough time to do another search for Luca, to dig deeper.

She went to the Dark Web. A deeply buried website briefly mentioned her brother. She read quickly, scanning the document. Luca had pissed the wrong people off. He'd slept with a capo's daughter and refused to make an honest woman of her. He'd then married another woman. The newlyweds had died in a car bombing on their way home from the wedding.

Her brother was dead. Dead for nearly a year.

Eva sat back in shock. She didn't feel a shred of pity for him. Instead, a wave of fear trickled through her. If Luca hadn't killed her family, who had?

A FEW HOURS LATER, with a ball cap pulled low and huge sunglasses on, Eva parked on the street outside the school in her new car—an environmentally friendly vehicle—something no self-respecting Malibu housewife would drive. It was a car that a Minnesota soccer mom would tool around in.

It was also a common disguise for nearly all the celebrities in Los Angeles when they tried to get about town incognito. If anyone thought she was in disguise, in L.A. it would be natural for them to assume she was some hot actress trying to keep a low-profile.

Eva held her binoculars up and pointed them at the windows of the library. She saw Krystal's blonde head bob by occasionally, until finally the lights went out. A few minutes later, she was tailing Krystal's massive, white Lexus SUV through the streets of Los Angeles, keeping far enough back to not draw attention or suspicion.

Soon, Krystal pulled up before a gated community. Damn it.

Eva pulled over to the side of the road and watched as Krystal and the guard had a brief conversation.

The gate clanked closed behind her vehicle.

Eva pulled into the driveway, stopping at the gate. The guard looked at her through the window.

"I'm here to see Krystal Diamond."

He frowned. "She didn't say anything about a visitor."

"That's odd," Eva said. "She wanted me to start coming to her house to do her weekly massage since she has to work late on Thursdays now—they changed the late day, I guess."

"She did mention that change," he frowned again. "Well, she just pulled into the community, so she's not at her house yet."

"Great. I was running a few minutes behind, so now I won't be late."

He stared at her for a second and then opened the gate.

Eva smiled. "Thanks. I'm Kim. I'll be coming on Thursdays from now on."

He nodded formally.

"Oh, one other thing," Eva said. "She told me the name of the community but forgot to give me the house number. We got busy talking about Patricia's party this Sunday."

Eva hoped by dropping the principal's name, she'd solidify her story even more.

"5407."

"Thanks."

Eva zipped in, watching in relief as the gate closed behind her. As soon as she was out of the guard's line of sight, she punched the accelerator.

A mile up the road, she spotted a sign for 5407 and a long, cobblestone driveway leading to a massive house perched on the edge of the Hollywood hillside.

She arrived in time to see the garage door closing. She pulled to the side of the driveway under a tree, hoping her dark vehicle would not attract attention as she surveyed the house. If Eva was right, Krystal was home alone. Yates and his father would be at karate class. She'd once heard Krystal saying that Thursday nights were her home spa and Real Housewives night because "the boys" were gone.

The house faced the east and had windows at the front and back, so even from where Eva was she could see the sun setting on the Pacific not far away. The view was spectacular. The plastic surgery business must be doing well.

At the same time, the glass house creeped her out. Anyone could see inside. The family must really trust that guard at the gatehouse and their neighbors to not come snooping around. Eva would never ever live in a house that exposed her that way, even if there hadn't been a decade-long hit out on her life.

Eva yanked off her hat and dark glasses and held the binoculars up to her eyes, pointing them at the various windows of the house. She spotted Krystal in an upstairs window stripping off her top.

Something caught Eva's eye toward the side of the house facing the small canyon. A figure emerged from the bushes to the south. The person had a lithe body and was dressed all in black with a black face mask. Eva saw the person had a gun. Her blood raced, and she instinctively reached for the dagger strapped to her back, but then her hand dropped. The gun in her ankle holster was what she really needed. She watched the figure creep around to the back of the house.

Eva opened her car door and slipped out, leaving the door open behind her. She ran toward the house, keeping her gaze trained on the floor-to-ceiling front windows that presented a view of the entire first level and then straight through the house and through the bank of windows facing west.

Within a few seconds, a dark form emerged on the back deck. Eva crept toward the front of the house, watching as the intruder boldly picked up a chair and smashed it through a back window. Eva jumped. Her eyes flicked up to the second story. She watched as Krystal first raced for the bedroom door and then jerked back toward the bed, scrambling for a cell phone.

Down below, the person's gloved hands chopped at the remaining fragments of glass still stuck in the frame until there was a large enough opening to step through.

Eva was sprinting now, racing toward the front of the house. Meanwhile, she saw the dark silhouette of the figure loping toward the staircase. At the front door, Eva smashed the window pane near the door with her gun. She reached in to unlock the door so she didn't have to worry about cutting herself on the jagged window edges.

Once inside, she raced toward the stairs, stooping in mid-run long enough to yank her pistol out of its ankle holster. She wished she'd brought more weapons. From the way the intruder moved and acted, Eva knew she was dealing with a professional. He knew what he was doing. He would be a formidable match.

As she crested the landing on the second floor, she paused, breathing heavily, and listening hard. Several doorways flanked the hall before her. From her earlier vantage point of the bedroom, Eva knew it was either the second or third door down. Holding the gun in front of her, she hugged the wall, creeping forward, eyes trained on the doors to her right.

She stepped into the master bedroom.

The masked figure held a knife to Krystal's throat. As soon as she saw Eva, Krystal began to cry.

"Eva! I swear I didn't mean it. Call your dog off. Please. I'm sorry. Please. Please." She was blubbering now. "I hit the silent alarm. The police will be here any second. I promise I won't say anything if you let me go. Just leave now. I'll tell them it was a false alarm. I promise.

Please don't kill me. Call him off. Eva! Please."

Up close, Eva realized the masked intruder was male.

Foolish woman. Now she would die. Eva didn't know if she had time to stop it now that Krystal had confessed to the police coming.

Eva met the eyes of the man in mask. They were dark, but that was all she could distinguish. But they also sent a clear message: he was going to kill Krystal, and he wanted Eva to watch.

"Drop the knife," Eva said. To her dismay, her arms were trembling. The man in black looked pointedly at the wildly shaking Ruger in her hands. The next few seconds came in snapshots—the slightest movement as his fingers tightened on the blade at Krystal's throat; Eva harnessing every ounce of her energy into her trigger finger; raising the gun steadily and quickly; squeezing the trigger smoothly; firing off two shots one after the other directly into the man's forehead; kneeling to tuck her gun back into her ankle holster.

Then everything sped up to double time—the masked man slumped to the ground in a heap, his knife clattering onto the marble floor; Krystal's mouth opening in a long blood-curdling scream; the sound of sirens in the distance.

Pushing Krystal out of the way, Eva knelt by the dead man and ripped the rubber mask off. She stared at a face she'd never seen before in her life.

Meanwhile, Krystal's wailing and weeping continued, and the sirens grew closer. Without a backward glance, Eva raced out of the room toward the stairs, jumped down six at a time, and then hurled herself out onto the back deck. She leaped off the side and raced into the bushes in the direction she'd seen the man come from just as the first squad car pulled into Krystal's driveway. She tumbled down the steep hill for about twenty feet until it leveled off. A small deer path led further downhill, so she sprinted down it, hoping it would lead her where she needed to go. Above, she heard shouting and more sirens.

Ninety yards away she saw it. A road. And the gleam of metal from a small, dark SUV. It was parked on a residential road below Krystal's house, outside of the gated community. Eva darted toward it, hoping her hotwiring skills from long ago would still work on a newer car. But no sooner had she thought that, than she saw the silhouette of a head in the driver's seat. She pulled up short, but only to reach down and take her gun back out of its holster. As she stood straight again, she readjusted her grip on the gun and headed straight for the vehicle at a sprint.

She was within fifteen feet of the SUV when the driver gunned the engine and peeled out, scattering gravel and dirt and dust.

Eva held the gun before her, tempted to fire at the receding vehicle, but was blinded by the dust cloud. It sent her into a coughing fit.

Instead, aware of the sirens just up the hill from her, she sprinted after the vehicle, keeping to the shoulder. About a quarter mile later, she saw what she needed: a driveway with a vehicle parked in it. Within seconds, she'd hotwired the minivan and roared off, heart pounding, with an eye on the rearview mirror.

She soon realized the gunman and his accomplice had planned their escape route well. They'd chosen that particular spot to park because the road was out of the gated community and led straight to a major artery in Los Angeles—the 405 freeway. Soon, Eva was on the freeway, blending into traffic and heading back to her new home. She tucked the stolen minivan into the garage and, after checking the security footage to make sure her home had remained unmolested, she stripped and stepped into the shower.

Although she didn't have blood or guts on her—only dirt and twigs stuck to her hair and clothing—she needed to wash the murder off. She hadn't killed anyone in more than a decade. And this kill might have been the wrong one. The figure in the SUV might have been the woman she was truly after. While she'd only seen the silhouette of a head through the vehicle's window, there was something strikingly familiar about the person—something about them that she knew, something she recognized.

If she was right, it had almost certainly been the woman who'd killed her family, and she had been this close to her. Eva swore and wanted to punch something. She'd killed the wrong person. There was no room for even the slightest miscalculation. Though she'd done it to save Krystal's life, Eva knew it had been a mistake.

She leaned her forehead against the shower wall, letting the scalding water pound down on her scalp, and realized she'd lost the taste for murder. What had once given her a sense of limitless power, now filled her with regret. In hindsight, she knew that under the same circumstances, she'd do it again. But she no longer took pleasure in taking a life. It had become so distasteful to her, she had to steady herself from collapsing onto the shower floor in a heap.

She told herself it would be different if it was a murder of vengeance but killing that masked man had left a bad taste in her mouth. She was questioning herself. Could she have shot to disable instead of kill? She didn't know. But what she did know was that after she avenged her family's murder, she'd turn herself in.

As she thought this, she batted away a small thought creeping into her mind—a nagging sense of doubt that whispered in her ear: You're weak. You've lost your edge. You won't be able to kill again. When you are faced with the woman who slaughtered your family, you will crumble. You will never avenge them. You will die in vain.

"STOP!" The word echoed in the bathroom. Swiping at her eyes, she realized she was overtired, dehydrated, hungry, and on the verge of delirium. But she didn't move. Instead, she stood there in the steamy shower, her face pressed against the slick tiles, and fought the urge to vomit. Finally, after some deep breathing exercises, she was able to finish washing herself.

It was only when she stood wrapped in a thick towel, shivering and teeth chattering, that she realized she'd been shaking nonstop since she stepped into the house.

13

"The blonde is alive. My man is dead. And Eva is underground."

He said it in an even tone and waited for Ludovicus "Luigi the Arm" Mazzo's reaction. And sure enough, the older man's displeasure could nearly be felt through the phone line even from more than 6,000 miles away.

"Cagacazzo!" The Arm did not sugarcoat his feelings about people who failed to follow his orders. He'd just called Vincenzo an incompetent idiot.

Vincenzo swallowed back his injured pride and tried to keep his tone matter of fact, without whining in justification.

"She showed up early. She killed my man. In front of the blonde."

The silence stretched on for a few long seconds before the man in Sicily spoke.

"This is good."

"But we failed."

"Maybe not."

The Arm's plan had been to lure Eva to the scene of the murder. The hitman had waited in the bushes until he saw Eva's car drive up.

The idea was as soon as the hitman did his job, he'd return to the car where Vincenzo would call 911 and report that Eva White had killed Krystal Diamond. There was no way Eva could escape. Even if she managed to drive away before the police arrived, the security guard at the gate would testify he saw her and her fingerprints would be all over everything, implicating her.

But everything had gone sideways. Eva had killed the hit man and escaped. That was fine. After all, Vincenzo had planned to take the hitman out himself after Krystal's murder. He didn't want to leave any witnesses behind.

But still, Vincenzo had made a mistake. He'd foolishly assumed Eva had grown soft over the years. That becoming a mother would've taken the blood-lust out of her. He was wrong. She was possibly more powerful than ever. Even more reason he should kill her outright instead of adhering to the Arm's plan. Because for some reason, the old man had convinced himself that Eva living with the massacre of her family—and being blamed for it—was the worst possible punishment he could exact upon her.

Vincenzo bit his tongue but was tempted to say, "Just because this is what you lived through does not mean it is worse than death."

But how did he really know? So instead of screaming into the phone, hurling accusations and arguments, Vincenzo simply asked,

"What now?"

"Wait for my instructions," the Arm said.

The line disconnected.

14

Eva slept for nine hours before she woke up, throat parched, weak, and nauseous. After gulping three glasses of water in the kitchen and wrapped only in the sheet from her bed, she saw the bowl of fruit left by the real estate agent. She stood at the counter and ate three oranges, two bananas, and an apple before she turned to the cupboards.

Bare.

She'd order food and have it left at the front gate. She needed to eat. She needed to build up her strength. Yesterday's mission had shown her that she had grown soft. If she hoped to avenge her family before she died, she had to return to the woman she'd been in Sicily.

Pumped up by the sugar rush from the fruit, Eva downed another glass of water and began her morning exercise routine.

It was a regimen she'd begun immediately upon arriving on American soil. She performed the exercises religiously each morning. Until this week, she'd only missed two mornings in ten years— once when the morning sickness she'd experienced with Lorenzo had been at its worst, and the other was the morning after her wedding when she and Matthew woke in Cabo San Lucas on their honeymoon.

"You must really love me," he said after she'd made love to him, showered, dressed, and grabbed her bag for them to head to the beach.

She turned and smiled. "Why do you say that? Obviously, I do." She held up her left hand, the wedding ring gleaming in the light, and fluttered it at him.

"I didn't think I'd ever see the day when you skipped your morning workout."

"Today, the first day I am Mrs. Eva White, is an exception. But it won't happen again. I'll be up early working out tomorrow while you're sleeping in." She laughed as she said it, and her tone was lighthearted, but she was dead serious.

He smiled but then grew somber.

He wrapped his arms around her from behind and kissed her neck before whispering in her ear, "I don't know why you need to keep your secrets from me, but I love you enough to trust that you have a good reason. Whatever it is, you know I will love you no matter what. I will also love you forever, even if you never tell me a single thing about your past. You know that."

Tears pricked her eyes. She turned in his arms and said, "Matthew, it's because I love you more than life itself that I can't share everything with you."

He stared at her for a second before answering, "I know."

It was the last time he'd brought up her past and her secrets. His trust in her had made her fall more deeply in love with him than she could've imagined possible.

That's why she had to avenge his murder. Her husband and children had been innocent. They had died for her sins.

She would never rest until she settled the score.

This burning desire propelled her through her grueling routine. Two hours later—after going through her Navy Seal workout of push-ups, sit-ups, pull-ups, dips and then an hour on the treadmill-

she was done and in the shower. This time she ended the scalding shower with a blast of cold water, counting until she'd stood under the icy needles for two full minutes.

After she was dressed, she sat cross legged on the wooden floor and meditated, then did some simple yoga stretches before opening her laptop and placing an order for food delivery. Fish. Vegetables. Fruit. Eggs. Nuts. Her body was her weapon, and she needed to fuel it properly for battle. She also ordered a yoga mat, black lingerie, five pairs of thick, black leggings, and five black long-sleeve shirts, work out gear, running shoes, a high-powered smoothie maker, and protein powder. She was in training.

Only when she had ordered what she'd need to survive for the next few weeks did she click over to the local news websites. Only two stations still had stories posted on her. The first one repeated old information. It hadn't been updated since the night before. But the second station had just been updated that morning. She clicked on the recorded video. It was about the incident at Krystal's house.

She knew killing the masked man with the knife had only solidified her standing as a suspect, and yet she still flinched seeing her honeymoon photo on the computer monitor. Hopefully, Krystal wasn't savvy enough to have noticed that she'd dyed her hair black.

The news anchor switched to footage of Krystal standing in front of her home. Repairmen in the background were replacing her windows.

"I talked her into letting me go," Krystal said into the camera. "She told him, the guy with the knife, to let me go, but then she shot him. Right in the head. Oh, my god. Oh, my god." Krystal was fanning herself, hyperventilating.

"It's okay Mrs. Diamond. Take your time," the reporter said, nodding sympathetically. "Were you the only one home at the time?"

Krystal ignored the question. "She killed a man right in front of me. In front of me. Dead. In my own bedroom. I'm being treated for post-traumatic stress disorder. I haven't slept or eaten a bite since then. I told my husband I can never sleep in this house again. We are selling our house. We are leaving immediately."

"Can you tell our viewers more about how the man was shot?"

"She did it while he was still holding me. I mean, maybe she was a bad aim and was aiming for my head. Why would she kill one of her own?"

"Can you think of a reason why she killed him?"

Krystal scrunched up her face, her turned up nose wrinkling.

"Maybe. I don't know."

"Did you say earlier he was holding a knife to your throat?"

"Yes. He could have sliced my throat open. What if he jerked from the gunshot and the knife went in me?"

The reporter looked at the camera. "When we asked police if Eva White was now a suspect in her family's slaying because of this recent incident, they would only say she's a person of interest. Ken."

The cameras cut back to a well-coifed man in the newsroom.

"Thanks, Belinda. Have they at least named Mrs. White as a suspect in the homicide at Mrs. Diamond's house?"

"No, Ken. They are continuing to call her a 'person of interest' in both crimes."

Fools. Eva clicked off the website in disgust. Maybe she should have let the witch die. Who was to say that Yates was better off with her alive. Maybe his life would've turned out better if his mother had died. Any mother like that would surely be poison to a child, wouldn't she?

But Eva knew she'd do it again. Every instinct in her directed her to protect the innocent. It was her mother's fault. Her mother had been the one to take in strays during Eva's childhood. Whether it was a cat with a litter of kittens or a neighborhood kid who was neglected at home. Eva's mother had raised her to believe that caring for the less fortunate and vulnerable was her duty in life.

Thinking of her mother sent a sharp bolt of pain behind Eva's eyes. She didn't even know if her mother were still alive. She'd once gone to the library and searched for information on her mother, looking in and around Rome, but nothing had come up in the search results.

Eva paced and prowled her new home. She was going to have to ditch the stolen car. On second thought, that would be too dangerous. She'd have to steal some license plates first and then switch them out before she could ditch the car. Meanwhile, she needed a set of wheels. But first she had to wait for the food delivery.

Restless, she moved every single piece of furniture out of the large living room—the couches, the tables, and the TV—and began practicing her Gladiatura Moderna routine.

She was a little rusty. The smooth and flowing moves required of the ancient knife-fighting, martial arts form eluded her on this day. She vowed to make it part of her daily workout until she regained the fluidity of her youth.

If she executed a move clumsily, she forced herself to repeat it. Over and over again.

She'd worked up a sweat again by the time her phone dinged, alerting her to the delivery waiting at the bottom of her driveway. Wiping the sweat off her face with a towel, she reviewed the security footage.

Everything had been done according to her directions. She'd have to risk driving the stolen van down her long driveway to pick up the delivery. But from what she'd seen reviewing surveillance camera footage at her front gate, traffic was rare. It looked like the two neighbors above her—one a doctor and, further up the road, a Hollywood executive—were not home often. The doctor, a woman who worked in the oncology department at USC, seemed to work twenty-four hour shifts. Her vehicle would leave and not return for a day, coming home in the morning and then staying put for another two days before leaving again for another twenty-four-hour period. Perfect. It looked like she had a maid service that came once a week, but it had been there the day before.

The Hollywood executive left his house around nine and returned by eight. Information she'd found online showed he was divorced. His wife lived nearby in an expensive Beverly Hill's home. A brief scan of the divorce papers showed he'd won joint custody of their one son, so Eva might expect to see the wife dropping the kid off occasionally. She wasn't sure.

Her recon showed that if she drove the minivan down to the gate to collect her supplies right now—at two in the afternoon—the chances of another vehicle going by were slim.

At the bottom of the driveway, Eva listened for any vehicles on the road. All she heard was the squawking of a flock of parrots in the trees above. That had always amazed her—how could there be wild parrots in Los Angeles? But there were. In Sicily, they'd had roaming packs of wild boar. Here they had wild parrots.

She pressed the gate open so she could load the packages and bags into the back of the minivan. She was almost done when a voice in her ear had her reaching for her gun.

Heart pounding, she whirled to see a boy on a bike.

"Whoa," he said, dropping his bike and running a few paces away when he saw the gun.

"Oh my God. I'm so sorry. You startled me," Eva said, heart pounding. Something about the boy reminded her of Lorenzo. For a second, she grew dizzy and had to grab hold of the side of the car, closing her eyes.

"I can tell," the boy said, giving her a wary look. "Are you okay?"

"Yes," Eva said, opening her eyes and trying to regain her composure.

"Hey, are you a cop?"

Eva felt her face grow hot. She tucked the gun back into her waistband and gave a slight nod. "I didn't mean to scare you. Just reflexes."

The boy stared at her. She looked down, reaching for the last bag, hoping he was buying her lie.

"Are you our new neighbor?"

She stood, holding the bag in front of her, and nodded without meeting his eyes.

He stayed silent.

Her heart was pounding. Did he recognize her from the news? "Do you have a badge?"

"I really don't think...." her voice trailed off. It would be better if he thought she was a police officer. "Can I see it?"

"I have to go." All she wanted was to get away from this boy. He looked to be about the same age as Lorenzo, and talking to him was like having someone stab a knife through her heart. Please leave.

"What's your name?"

Why was this kid out running around by himself in the middle of the day anyway?

"How old are you?"

"Ten."

Jesus Christ. He was the same age as Lorenzo. And he was grilling her. She pretended to arrange the grocery bags in the back of the vehicle, trying to stand in front of the license plate number in case this kid was a lot savvier than he let on.

"Why aren't you in school?" She tried to sound gruff. "Isn't it against the law to be truant?"

He scoffed. "It's spring break. Duh."

"That's right," Eva said, smoothly. But inside she crumpled. She'd planned to take the kids to San Diego for spring break. "Where's your dad?"

"At work."

"He lets you stay home alone?"

"Yeah." Then he frowned. "Since you're a cop, can you help me find something out about someone?"

Eva narrowed her eyes. She didn't answer, but that didn't stop the boy from continuing to speak.

"You see my dad? He's not my real dad."

Although Eva wanted to run far away from this boy, she waited. Being around him hurt too much. He even had a similar haircut and wore the same scruffy Converse sneakers that Lorenzo had. But at the same time, she yearned to hear him speak. So she listened. It wasn't his fault that speaking to him felt like a knife in the heart. He was obviously lonely or he wouldn't still be here talking to her.

"I want to find my real dad. If I give you, like, some of my spit, can you help me find my real dad?"

At first Eva balked. What the hell? She wouldn't even be living here long enough for the DNA results to come back. This kid was awfully ballsy. But then again, she liked that.

"I don't know. Don't you like living with your dad? The one you have now?" Her voice was soft now.

He nodded so hard his ball cap nearly came off. A long lock of brown hair fell over his eyes and his freckled nose. His eyes were wide pools of chocolate brown. They were lighter than Lorenzo's dark orbs.

"He thinks I don't know. But I heard my mom talking."

"What if he doesn't even know? Would you risk breaking his heart like that?" Eva realized she was talking to him like an adult. She decided to pull back.

The boy swallowed, his Adam's apple bobbing. "It's just that he's really sick. Like he's not at work today. He's at the doctor. He thinks I don't know. But he has to go get stuff for cancer. He doesn't want me to know. But I found out. I saw the report the doctor gave him. I know how to find things like that on the computer. We share an account on the cloud. He doesn't think I know how to do stuff like that.. I think he might die. And I can't go live with my mother. She hates me."

"I doubt that."

He shrugged. "Believe what you want. She does." He said it so matter-of-factly, looking down at his sneakers that Eva believed him.

And her heart broke a little.

He picked his bike back up and straddled it. "I gotta go."

Eva made a decision. As much as part of her never wanted to see or speak to another ten-year-old boy again, this kid obviously needed her and needed her help. She'd have to set aside her own pain.

"I'll get a test. And let you know when it gets here."

He smiled for the first time. "Thanks," he said. "Hey, what's your name?"

She stared at him for a second and then answered, "Lucia." "Loo-chee-a?"

"Yes." She smiled. "What's your name?"

"Dolan."

"Nice to meet you, Dolan."

She turned and closed the gate, watching his slender figure as he stood on his bike to gain the momentum to peddle up the steep hill. She watched him until he disappeared before she got into the minivan.

15

SICILY

The golden light of morning filled the bed chamber. The fresco on the wall opposite the bed always gave him a sense of security, wealth, and power —and made him super horny. He might be in his sixties, but he would never take those little blue pills. Not when he could wake every morning and be turned on by the orgy playing out on his wall.

Ludovicus "Luigi the Arm" Mazzo had bought this crumbling villa with its location high on a hill for two reasons: he could spot any enemy heading his way and for the frescos that covered several walls of the house. From the outside, the villa looked worn down and ordinary, but inside, spectacular frescos adorned the ceilings and walls. But the best one of all was in the master bedroom. An ancient bacchanalia scene. It never failed to give him a massive hard-on.

As he sat up in bed, propped on several silk-clad pillows, he reached under the covers and fumbled for his member, making sure he was rock solid hard before he rolled over toward Francesca.

Her red hair splayed across the peach pillowslip, and one massive, soft, white breast stuck out where the covers had fallen away.

Just then the phone rang. He groaned. It was from America.

"What?" He snarled the word into the phone.

"I saw you called."

"That was last night."

Francesca stirred beside him; one long-lashed eye opening.

"Should I call back later?" the voice in his ear said.

"Yes!" He practically screamed the word and threw the phone down, reaching for his wife's bare breast. She turned away.

"Isn't that thing in America over anyway."

She never liked to talk about his business directly, only in veiled terms.

"It's not over," he said, growing even more irritated that his morning love session was being overridden by talk about her. Would he ever rid himself of her?

"Haven't you done enough?" Francesca asked.

"Woman," he said. "You don't understand these matters."

"I think I do." She threw back the peach silk sheet and reached for the gunmetal gray cigarette case on the nightstand. She tapped out a slim cigarette and stuck it between her voluptuous, full lips. Before she could reach for her matches, he held a flame at the tip of her cigarette.

"Amore mio," he said.

She sighed, enjoying this fleeting moment of power and pampering. But she was wary. It wouldn't last long. The sweet, remorseful part of the cycle of violence never did. The morning after he beat her to a pulp, he showered his affection on her. He'd spent most of the

night weeping at her feet, hugging her knees, promising to never lift a finger against her again.

"How do I know you meant what you said. Last night?" She swallowed as she spoke.

"Tesoro mio." My treasure. "Mi dispiace." I'm sorry. "I will do better. I will be better. I promise. You know you are my queen."

She waited to answer until she had inhaled, turning her gaze to the sweeping panoramic view out the floor-to-ceiling windows. The grapes were coming in fine this year. Far in the distance, she could see the Tyrrhenian Sea twinkling. Somewhere across the hills to the west was the house where they had met. She had been a teenage prostitute, escaping an abusive father and trying to save money to go to the mainland. He'd taken one look at her and beaten her pimp to death, then brought her to this villa where he'd pampered her for years.

Although in that first encounter, she'd seen his violence, he'd never been violent with her. Well, except a tiny bit in bed. And she'd liked it.

From the very beginning, there had been an extraordinary sexual chemistry between them, and this often made up for the marriage's other shortcomings, such as their inability to conceive a child and the fact that their luxurious lifestyle was financed by the blood of others.

For much of their marriage, only the sex had been tinged with violence. If she ever said something that hurt or asked him to stop, he always had. Until recently.

He'd first raised his hand against her a few weeks before. She was a cunning and intelligent woman and looked at the incidents logically, not emotionally. She had escaped a fate worse than death when he rescued her from the pimp. She was forever in his debt, so she had forgiven the first few times. But despite his weeping, remorse, and promises, the beatings continued. And she thought she might know why.

"I'm a woman," she said. "I say she's been punished enough. Let her live in her own misery—knowing her family died because of her own actions."

"It's not enough."

She inhaled before speaking. Lately, since their relationship had morphed into something unstable, she carefully measured her words before speaking. She never knew if what she said would trigger his rage. But if there were ever a time to speak her mind, it was now— when he was ashamed and remorseful.

"My husband, what happened last night..." she paused as he winced. "What I've realized is that it all started a few weeks ago when this thing from America started to move forward. I can't help but think there is some connection. That is why I ask you to let it go now, so we can go back to the way it was."

"There is no connection. Impossible." He sat up, his face turning cold as stone.

"What do you want?" she said.

He reached over, his eyes hooded, and stroked her. A guilty lust raced through her. A few incidents of domestic violence didn't blot out years of hot sex, she told herself. But deep inside, she knew she was justifying the way her body betrayed her—leaning into his touch and moaning.

"I want her utterly destroyed."

As he said it, he grunted and flipped her over. In one smooth move, he entered her from behind without warning, expending his anger with each thrust. It didn't take a degree in psychology for Francesca to know that he was imagining that the woman groaning with pleasure under him was Eva Lucia Santella.

16

Los Angeles

Eva couldn't help herself. As soon as the noon news came on, she sat glued before the large-screen TV, flipping through the channels, looking for any stories about her and her family.

She told herself it would help her find the killer and that she was searching for more breadcrumbs or clues the woman might have left for her. Because the card on Krystal's dashboard had been meant strictly for Eva. And it had been done during the live news shot.

The news crews were back at the school. The interview had already begun. It was the principal of the Rembrandt Academy speaking into a grouping of microphones taped to a school podium in the library.

"We don't intend to let this tragedy affect our school," she said. "It's a shame that some parents feel that way."

"Are you saying that Nikos Alexopoulos withdrew his son from the school because of the slayings?"

The woman bit her lip. Her cheeks grew slightly pink. "I do not know why Ricardo is no longer at our school."

Eva sat back, frowning. Did that mean that Nikos thought she had killed her family? Then she realized, why wouldn't he? Everyone else did.

A reporter with giraffe legs and long, flowing light brown hair asked the next question. "Is it true that several families have withdrawn their children, not just Mr. Alexopoulos."

Now the principal was visibly flustered. A small drop of sweat dripped down one brow.

"I am not permitted to release the enrollment statistics at our academy. You will have to talk to the board of directors about that. I held this press conference to let everyone know that despite the terrible attack on our librarian Krystal Diamond, plans for the annual fundraiser are on track and on schedule. And we are still looking for donations—"

Eva was about to turn the TV off when the station cut to the newsroom.

"We are interrupting our coverage at the Rembrandt Academy because there is a press conference at the police station right now regarding the Malibu Colony Slayings."

Eva stared. Her family's murder had a name. A nickname. It made her want to vomit.

But then it got worse.

The public information officer, a short guy in an ill-fitting suit, came to the podium. She closed her eyes and tuned out most of what he was saying about how the medical examiner's office was still conducting its investigation into the cause of death of the three people and so on. But then she heard him introduce someone else. Detective Jay Collins.

Her eyes flicked back open. It was the detective assigned to the case. She needed to call him. She needed to point him in the right direction. She needed his help to find her family's killer. She studied him, leaning in toward the TV. He wore a tight black T-shirt under a well-cut blazer as he stood in front of the podium on the steps of the police station. He sported aviator sunglasses and had silver streaks in thick black hair pushed back from his face.

"THANK YOU ALL FOR COMING. We have some new information on the White family murders."

Eva sighed in relief. At least the cops weren't using that other stupid name that reduced her family's lives to a true crime show title.

"We are asking the public's help in locating the following vehicle, which we believe Mrs. White may be driving."

He reeled off the make, model, color, and license plate number of the minivan sitting in Eva's garage. Damn. Then he showed a picture taken from a traffic camera of Eva in the minivan getting onto the freeway near Krystal's house. Ouch.

"We also believe Ms. White now has dark hair, not the lighter color we had in a previous photo."

Eva was outraged. When did she lose her married "Mrs." She wasn't a Ms. But then her entire body felt deflated. She lost that title when they assumed she killed her family. Well, that was not okay with her She would think of herself as Mrs. White until the day she died. Nobody could take that away from her.

The reporters continued to volley questions at the detective.

"Have you named her as a suspect?"

The detective didn't flinch, but he did pause before saying firmly, "Mrs. White remains a person of interest. We would like to question her about what happened that day." Again, he reeled off a tip line number where callers could remain anonymous. Eva memorized it. She wondered how "anonymous" it really was.

There were murmurings among the reporters and then another reporter spoke up.

"What else can you tell us about the Malibu Colony Killer?"

"We will release more information as it becomes available."

The detective left the podium and stepped into the front door of the police station without another word.

Eva took the burner phone out onto the back deck. She stood against the rail and punched in the number. She wasn't going to bother to try to hide her voice. She wanted them to know who was calling. She wasn't worried about them tracing the call. Her system was flawless. Any traces on the number would lead techs on a wild goose chase, sending them around the world and then landing right back in the Malibu house where she used to live. It would probably send them scrambling with lights and sirens to the beach house, which was a waste of their time and resources.

She dialed.

"Malibu Police Tip Line."

Good. Not a recording. A live person.

"This is Eva White." She waited a few seconds for the name to set in.

"Oh. Oh. Oh!"

"I need to speak to Detective Collins. Hurry because I'll hang up if he's not on the line in ninety seconds."

"Stand by."

Eva looked at her watch. "Detective Collins." Seventy seconds.

"I need your help."

"If you come in, we can talk."

"That's not what I mean. I don't have time for that nonsense," Eva said. "I didn't kill my family. I can explain. But I need your help finding the killer."

He was quiet for a second and then said, "Go on."

"Do you believe me?"

"The evidence doesn't support what you're saying. The video. There's also the insurance policy. Shall I go on?" "What insurance policy?" He paused.

Eva swore softly. She had no idea. God damn it, Matthew. I told you not to do that! I told you we'd take care of ourselves.

She was filled with fury that her husband's act of generosity and love was now considered a solid motive for murder.

"Never mind," she said.

"There are a lot of factors that don't support your innocence," he said.

"There's no time stamp on the video. Is that normal? Ask the security company about that? And the killer only shoots out the cameras afterward. If I were the killer, why wouldn't I have disabled the cameras immediately? Why would I wait and let it film the murders? The killer disabled the video then so it wouldn't show me coming home from the school and finding my family." Eva paused.

"And there's more. She's baiting me."

"She?"

"The killer. The woman who looks like me and murdered my family. The woman who sent the man to kill Krystal Diamond."

"What?" He sounded interested now. She heard him whispering to someone else.

"That's sloppy," she said.

"Huh?" He was taken off guard.

"You should know better. You won't be able to trace this call."

He gave a small laugh. "We've been tracing it from the second you called."

He was still trying to keep her on the line.

"I can tell you right now that when you trace this call it will first take you to a location far away—let's say Helsinki and then maybe bounce to some island maybe, Mauritius. And then maybe it will hit a few European cities before careening over to let's say, Alaska, and maybe down to Winnipeg and finally landing at 47890 Malibu

Colony Road."

"That's your address."

"Very astute."

"Are you at your house?"

"No," she sighed. "I can see now that I'll have to prove to you I'm not lying."

She could hear him scribbling on a piece of paper.

"Go ahead and send your team to the house in Malibu. I hope that there's a squad nearby, so we can get all this over with."

"All what over with?"

"You not believing me."

She heard muffled voices as if his palm were over the phone.

"Okay, back at you," he said.

"You still don't believe me when I say you're wasting your time going to my house."

"Listen, I don't know you from Adam. You could be loony as they come. Right now, all I know is that there is a video of a woman with your spitting image killing an entire family and then looking right up at the camera. And you stand to gain quite a substantial sum of money from your husband's death. What would you think if you were in my shoes?"

A hot, dry wind had kicked up and was blowing her hair in front of her eyes. The Santa Anta winds. They were an L.A. legend. They'd been known to drive the most mild-mannered person into a frenzy— sometimes even into a murderous rage. Joan Didion had written about it best. When Eva came to

California, she'd devoured everything Didion had published about the Golden State. For a second, she forgot about the detective on the other end of the line and blinked to fight back tears remembering her first days with Matthew in California.

"What do you suggest?" His voice startled her.

"That you believe me. That you realize the killer is baiting me, taunting me, trying to draw me out. She wanted me to go to Krystal's house. She left me a clue. On the news. That's why I was able to get there in time to save Krystal."

"Back up. You went there to save Krystal?"

"Yes."

"But here's the part where your story falls apart. While you were there, you killed a man."

"Well, yeah," Eva said. "What did you want me to do? Let him slice her throat?"

That shut him up. She stared out at the Los Angeles basin, her blood starting to boil with anger and frustration.

"Please, Mrs. White, do us both a favor and turn yourself in. Come in and we can discuss all this in person. You can tell me everything. I promise you will be safe."

"Turn myself in while the woman who killed my family roams free? Forget it," she said. "Go waste your time at my Malibu beach house. If you want to listen to me, you can call this number back. It's untraceable. Good day, detective."

She hung up and glared at the phone. The wind was whipping and howling in the canyon, sending a chill through her body. Something about it was foreboding. She didn't know why. It didn't make sense that wind, on a brilliant, golden day, would be ominous. But it was. It was as if the wind was warning her. Leave. Run away. Forget about vengeance. Run for your life.

No. Her life would have been without meaning if she didn't avenge her family.

It was the only thing left worth living for.

17

The burner phone she'd used to call Detective Collins woke her early the next morning. A number with an L.A. area code appeared on the screen. The detective was the only one who had this number. She held it up to her ear without speaking.

"I wanted you to have my personal number," Collins said. "This is my cell phone. You know...in case you change your mind and want to turn yourself in."

"Did you go to the house and see I was telling the truth?" He sighed loudly.

"I'll take that as a yes," Eva said, sitting up in bed and running a hand through her tangled hair to get it off her face. "Do you believe me now? Can we quit all these games and work together to find the monster who killed my family?"

"I just can't get past that video footage."

"So, you still think I'm lying," Eva said, standing and wrapping a blanket around her as she made her way into the kitchen.

"No."

"Okay then, so you think I'm crazy, delusional?" He gave a short bark of a laugh.

"You might think is funny, but this is my life."

He was silent for a second and then said, "My apologies. I was laughing because I don't think you're crazy or delusional. In fact, I think just the opposite. I would have to say I've never spoken to a saner-sounding, intelligent, witty, and interesting murder suspect in my life."

Eva's mouth dropped open.

"You have my number if you want to arrange to turn yourself in."

"Wait. Don't you dare hang up." Eva said. She was fuming with anger. "Why should I turn myself in? So you can grill me until I offer a false confession? I've heard what you guys do."

The detective gave a long sigh and then said, "Turn on the news." She did.

With horror, she watched the news station anchor announce that an arrest warrant had been issued for Eva White in connection with the homicide at Krystal Diamond's house.

"Mrs. White," he said. "Even you don't deny that you killed that man in Mrs. Diamond's house. That makes you a murder suspect. My job is to arrest you. Once I do, we can talk and figure out if maybe there were extenuating circumstances. There are all sorts of options. A plea deal? Self-defense? Who knows. But by not turning yourself in, you've given me no choice but to issue that arrest warrant."

Her anger flared. Why was she wasting her time talking to a detective who was playing with her, leading her on, trying to get her to slip and confess to a murder she didn't commit?

"Good luck finding the woman who killed my family," Eva said. "But know this and be warned—I'm going to find her first, and my justice won't be quite as lenient as yours."

She hung up and then chucked the phone across the room where it landed on the bed and skidded off onto the floor. She was shaking and furious. She had good instincts about people and thought the detective had believed her and might possibly even help her. She was wrong. Obviously, she was on her own. The detective could go screw himself. She'd find the killer first and make her pay. Game on, Detective Collins.

Meanwhile, she'd wait for another clue. If the detective really thought she was the killer, he wouldn't be paying attention enough to see it himself. At the very least, the clue, like the playing cards, might not mean anything to him. That was her advantage, and she intended to make the most of it.

Staring at the TV, she realized she needed to start taping the newscasts so she could replay them and look for clues. She set up her laptop to do so and then scrolled the major L.A. TV station's websites. They each had news of her arrest warrant. For some reason, news about her—even in a city with as many murders as L.A. had—was a top-read story.

Murders happened every day in Southern California. But because the victims were rich and white and lived in Malibu, her family's slayings were front and center.

Her own skin was olive. Not alabaster, but not super dark, either. And yet, she knew that once upon a time in America, Italians were not considered white. And there were some pockets of society who still felt that way.

Her son Lorenzo had inherited her darker skin and black eyes and black hair, but Alessandra was like her father, fair of skin and hair. No pictures of her family had been on the news yet. Eva thought she might not be able to bear seeing their little faces on a TV screen for the world to gawk at.

Listening to the news stories was painful, but she knew she needed to watch them, scan them for another clue. But there was nothing.

She turned the TV off. Time to work out. She had to keep up her strength. After making herself a green smoothie with protein powder, Eva spent the next four hours exercising and doing her Gladiatura Moderna martial-arts routine, feeling the cold metal of her daggers become an extension of her body, just like when she was in top form in Sicily so many years ago. It was coming back to her, and soon the movements would be automatic. That's where she needed to be— where it was all muscle memory and didn't require any conscious thought.

After, she showered and pulled a stool up to the bar and nibbled.

on almonds and drank another thirty-two ounces of water. She grabbed her laptop and opened a file and dictated what would become her daily routine. When she came face-to-face with the killer, she wanted to be in prime form. She didn't want there to be any chance of the woman escaping injured but with her life.

Eva laid out a diet, exercise, and sleep schedule.

Her training meant eating for strength and energy. Working out for four to six hours a day. Sleeping ten hours. It would make the days pass until she got the clue, she knew the killer would plant for her.

She figured it would take her at least ten days to condition herself. But the clue came the next morning.

It was the cute Latina reporter from the first news story at the school. Eva liked her, mainly because she'd seemed exasperated with Krystal during that first interview.

And the killer must have liked her as well because the clue was sent directly to her.

The Latina was at the newsroom reporting from a desk.

"We received a letter today that is purportedly from Eva White."

Eva froze, the remote control extended in front of her, still pointing at the TV as she stood there.

"We reported this information to the police department," she said. "They asked us not to share it publicly, but Eva White asked us to, saying that more people would die if we didn't do as she asked. We met with our station executives and attorneys and decided that it was in the public's best interest for us to follow the instructions left for us in the note."

Eva was outraged. The killer claimed the note was from her?

"Eva White asked us to share the note in its entirety, so we've decided to do that. Please be advised this is not appropriate for children."

The news reporter read the note at the same time it appeared on the screen. It was a printout with typed words.

"I cannot continue to live a life of privilege in my extravagant Malibu home, a life of lies, knowing the sins of which I am guilty. I was an assassin in my former life. My family did not know. I am willing to sacrifice more innocent lives in order to make the details of my many sins publicly known. There is so much blood on my hands already, another life or two won't make a difference to me. While the police are busy holding press conferences, I will be out here tying up loose ends before I atone for my sins and accept the punishment that is my due."

Eva tried not to let her fury cloud her thoughts. Stay calm, Santella. Where was the clue? What was it?

A male reporter gave an exaggerated sigh. "It sure looks like a confession, doesn't it Belinda?"

She gave him a rueful look, as if she were on Eva's side. "Unfortunately, it does look that way." She straightened the papers on her desk. "We've asked the police department for comment, but they informed us the note will be addressed at the press conference they already had scheduled for this afternoon."

"The police had this conference scheduled before the note was received, what do you think they are going to announce?" he asked.

Belinda shook her head. "At this point, I really can't say, but I would not be surprised if another arrest warrant is issued for Ms. White and they plead for her to follow through and turn herself in. What I find really interesting is that she admits to being an assassin. There's no other way to interpret that besides assuming she is a serial killer, which is very disturbing."

Eva clicked the TV off and logged onto the station's website. Good. They'd posted the note. What a bunch of idiots.

In Sicily, she was a mob boss who killed to maintain order. Some might call her an assassin. But she didn't do it for hire. She did it to protect the poor and innocent from greedy, evil men taking advantage of the helpless. And she'd never killed a woman. Or a child.

She re-read the note.

She examined each word. Each word meant something. The note was crafted as a clue. She just had to figure it out. After re-reading it a dozen times, Eva came to a few conclusions:

The killer was from Sicily. Her family was murdered because she'd killed —or ordered the death of—somebody in particular when she was a mob boss. That was a major clue. She made a list of all her victims and then put lines around them leading to all the family, friends, lovers, and business acquaintances that she could remember. By the time she was done, she had more than seventy-five names. And those were just the people she remembered or knew. Maybe some man she'd killed had a sister or niece or child she hadn't known about who had found her in America and sought to avenge his death?

The next part Eva thought was interesting was that there was only one location named. For some reason, the person had avoided referencing Italy or Sicily. But the note clearly mentioned one place: Her Malibu home.

It was so obvious that at first that she doubted it—the note was a direction invitation for her to go to the beach house.

During the press conference. It was suddenly crystal clear.

It was sooner than she expected, but she was ready.

She dressed in tight black pants, knee-high black boots with a thick tread, and a tight black top, and pulled her hair back in a tight ponytail. A halter that fit across her back would hold the two long dueling swords she'd put in her duffel bag. She strapped a dagger to the inside of her right boot and tucked a small pistol in a custom-made holster in the other. She had a small shoulder holster for her other gun. For good measure, she grabbed her burner phone—the one that contained Detective Collins's number—before she stepped into the garage.

Two miles down the road, she pulled onto a sleepy road and parked the stolen minivan under a leafy tree. She slipped into a burgundy SUV nearby and, within minutes, drove away with that one. She waited until she was at a hotel near LAX before she swapped out the SUV for a Suburban in a hotel parking garage. Then at LAX long-term parking she found the most beat-up, rusted heap she could find and drove that to her Malibu neighborhood.

Instead of parking on her street, she pulled into a public parking lot connected to a beach swim area. Too late, she realized she'd missed an important aspect of her planning—maintaining a low profile while walking down the beach to her old home. Dressed as she was—like a warrior about to go into battle—she'd stand out among the surf and beach crowd. She sat in the driver's seat staring at the beachgoers before she came up with the solution.

Waiting until the parking lot was empty and everyone had walked down to the beach, she stripped to her black underwear. She stuck her clothes and weapons into the duffel bag.

Then, in her black underwear and black bra, she grabbed a ratty towel out of the back seat of the car and wrapped it in a sarong, pulled her dark sunglasses down, and slung the duffel bag over her shoulder. Just another sun worshipper looking for a spot to camp out on the beach for the day.

She passed by all the other beachgoers without too much notice, if you didn't count the men ogling her body. She gave them a small upturn of her lips. All they would remember was a woman with curves walking on the beach in her bikini who had smiled at them.

When she got within two houses of her own, she turned up the beach and stepped through a small gate. Her neighbors two houses down, the Camdens, were gone for the season. They only stayed in their Malibu house in the winter. As soon as March hit, they headed to the French Riviera. Eva broke into their house and changed, tucking her long swords into her halter. Before leaving, she grabbed a pair of binoculars on the ledge that the couple used for whale watching.

Climbing to the fourth floor, Eva was glad for the first time that the Camden's had the tallest house on the beach. When she'd first moved in, she'd been irritated that another house could easily see into her third-floor bedroom. But after she met the couple, she felt better. They were elderly and harmless. The first time she'd been invited to their house, she'd done a little recon and found that this small study on the fourth floor offered the best views of her house. From here, one could see right into her master bath, but only a blank wall. The master bedroom wasn't visible.

She trained the binoculars on her house. She lowered them to get a view of the driveway. No cars. So far, so good. She could see the beginning of the gated driveway. The gate was closed. Police tape was strung across the front door, and other pieces of the yellow plastic hung across the doors to the back deck, the service room door, and the door to the garage. She was relieved to see they were unbroken. Anybody who might have forced their way inside would most likely have torn the plastic or at least stretched it out.

Although it hadn't been her first plan, Eva decided to first check inside her house and make sure the killer wasn't already holed up inside. Then, once she cleared it and possibly set a few traps, she would retreat back to the Camden's study where she'd wait for the killer to arrive. Once that happened, she'd break into her own home through a secret passageway accessible only from the beach level. The panel door looked like part of the wall. A small staircase led directly to her safe room. It would give her a chance to take the killer by surprise from inside the house. It wasn't a foolproof plan, but it would have to do.

As she crept out the Camden's side door, she tucked her cell phone deep into her boot. As she walked past, Eva hoped that the Nelsons, in the house between, were gone for the day. Both parents worked, and the kids were in grade school, so unless something unusual was happening that day, the house would likely be empty.

She gave a quick glance through the windows as she passed, but the house looked deserted. Once safe in the shadows under her own deck, she felt for the panel that triggered the secret door to open. She stepped inside the cool darkness and pushed the button for the panel door to close. Heart pounding, she waited in the dark and listened. She didn't hear anything unusual, so she crept up the dark staircase.

At the top, she felt the door to the safe room. She pressed her ear against the door and listened intently. She didn't hear anything that alarmed her, so she pushed another button. The door slid open silently. Her safe room had been trashed and stripped. Bare wires hung everywhere, and the door to her closet was wide open. She quickly stepped to one side, taking her gun out of the holster. She angled herself against the wall and listened. When she didn't hear anything, she crept toward the opening and peered out. Most of her clothes had been torn from the hangers and lay in a pile on the floor of the closet. The walk-in closet door was open, showing a glimpse of the master bedroom. She waited, watching and listening, before stepping into her closet, her gun held before her. She kept her eyes trained on the doorway to the master bedroom, pressed herself to one side, and silently made her way forward. She crouched at the doorway and scanned the room before stepping inside, assuring it was empty.

The covers had been torn off the large bed, and the mattress was askew. All her toiletries had been swept off the dresser onto the floor. Some perfume and cosmetic bottles had shattered, leaving an odd potpourri of both fresh and exotic scents in the air. A framed photograph of a street scene Matthew had taken during their trip to Cuba lay shredded on the floor by the bed. Clothing was dumped from drawers.

But her focus was on the door to the hall. Keeping her back to one wall, she silently glided forward. Once she reached the doorway, she again crouched before sticking her head out briefly, scanning quickly, before jerking it back in. Nothing. She rose and, gun first, stepped into the hall. The master bedroom was at one end of the hall, so keeping her back to it, she padded toward the children's rooms.

As soon as she reached Alessandra's doorway, she froze. Her heart thudded in her chest. Her mouth had grown dry and her legs weak. Her gun hand trembled. She closed her eyes for a second. She couldn't do it. But she had to. Taking a breath, she gently pushed the door open and glanced inside.

She could see immediately the room was clear, and the door to the adjoining bathroom was shut.

Like the master bedroom, Alessandra's room had been trashed. It seemed like way more destruction than what detectives investigating a homicide would leave behind. Why would they rip posters off the wall? It made Eva's blood boil as she took in the scene: dresser drawers yanked out and dumped, items swept off the dresser onto the floor.... Swallowing hard, Eva knew she had to get away from the bedroom or she would collapse in grief and fury. When she peered in Lorenzo's room, she saw the same. Again, she choked back her emotions. Later. Later she could think about how horrific it was to be in this house. Later in her prison cell.

The upstairs bathrooms were also clear, as was Matthew's study and the children's playroom. A week ago, a massive table held Legos on one end and a half-completed puzzle of Europe on the other. Now, everything was scattered on the floor. An old-fashioned arcade game that once stood in a corner was upended; the screen cracked.

Eva heard a slight sound and stepped back out of the room, gun before her, heart racing. But then she realized what the click was—an automatic timer that switched off the heater. She'd set it to turn the heat down when she was the only one home—after Matthew had gone to work and the children were at school.

She'd wanted the home toasty on cold mornings while everybody got ready, but once she was home alone, she could simply pull on a sweater if she was chilly. Matthew had told her not to worry about it —they had more money than they could spend in ten lifetimes. But her frugal ways, stemming from growing up in a poor country —eating panzanella salad to use up stale bread, taking in her brother's old pants so they would fit her, and reusing coffee grounds—were forever instilled in her. Even though her family was one of the richest in her country, frugality was part of the Sicilian DNA.

That's why the claim that she'd killed her family for the insurance money was so ludicrous. Absurd.

She brushed that thought away and made her way downstairs. Her heart clenched when she saw the foyer where Matthew's body had been. A dark stain had congealed.

Good God! Nobody had cleaned up the blood. She leaned her head against the wall at the bottom of the stairs, suddenly dizzy with grief. But then she remembered her task—searching the house for a killer who might be lying in wait. She jerked her head upright and lifted the arm holding the gun.

Her eyes flickered to what she could see of the first floor, which was most of it, since it had an open layout to assure that every room had a view of the bank of windows revealing blue sky and gray ocean.

From the foyer, she could see a little bit into the family room.

She'd save that for last and try to steel herself first. After searching all the other rooms on the downstairs level, she stepped toward the family room. As she got close to the large opening, she realized she'd be able to see most of it without actually stepping inside.

Once she was close enough to see the entire room, she scanned it as quickly as she could, her eyes skimming over the blood on the floor and couch. Don't go there. No. Not now. No.

It was the last room. The house was clear.

She stumbled to the stairs feeling sick and desperate. Her instinct was to get as far away from the first floor as possible. The horrors of that day kept flashing in her mind. Alessandra. Lorenzo. Matthew. Blood. Her entire life was destroyed.

She'd held it together for the past few days, but suddenly the devastation of losing everything she loved hit her at once.

Before she realized it, she was in the master bedroom, breathing hard, disoriented and dizzy. She leaned against one wall, weak with grief, trying to stop hyperventilating. Her arm with the gun dropped to her side. She squeezed her eyes shut trying to get it together. Breathe, she told herself.

A small sound, barely a whisper, came from just inches away.

She froze.

Her eyes flicked open.

A person in a rubber mask and rubber body suit stood before her holding a gun inches from her nose.

18

Los Angeles

Before she could react in any way, the masked figure's other arm came up out of nowhere and Eva felt a sharp prick in her neck. She flailed, but her body turned almost instantly to mush, sinking into the carpet. She tried to speak but only spluttered some saliva. Her mouth fell open like a fish sucking for air. Her vision whirled. The masked face peered down at her, multiplying and blurring. She was lifted up and placed on the bed. A gloved finger closed her eyes, and she lost the ability to open them again.

SHE WOKE to someone holding up the back of her head and pressing the lip of a cup to her mouth. She drank greedily, trying to quench her cotton mouth and swollen tongue.

Her arms and legs seemed paralyzed. Then she realized she could twitch them, but little else. As she gulped the rest of the water, her gaze landed on her captor. The eyes peering at her through the mask were unreadable. Black. Flat.

Then the cup was gone and the hand behind her neck disappeared. Her head flopped down hard on the mattress making her blink. "Who are you?" the words came out garbled, thick on her tongue.

She watched the figure stand and put the cup on the dresser next to a few gallon jugs of water. It was a man, she realized. Without a doubt. She could even see the groin area clearly through the rubber suit.

"Who?" Her voice cracked. Her lips were suddenly dry again.

The man turned his back to her and rummaged in a duffel bag. He tossed something pale her way that landed with a thud on her chest. It was followed by a beige furry thing that landed on top of it. She looked down and saw the fur was actually a wig. When she shifted, it slithered onto the bed, revealing the paler, slippery item. For a few seconds, she stared at it in disbelief before realizing what it was.

A silicon mask. It looked female with pink pouty lips. With his back to her, the man stood in front of her dresser watching her in the mirror.

"You son of bitch." She spit the words out. They sounded like a croak. He nodded his head slightly in acknowledgment.

Then she realized what he was doing. She could see it in the mirror—he was sharpening something. A dagger. One of hers.

Fear spiked through her, but only momentarily.

Whatever he had injected into her neck had knocked her out, but how long had it been? A few hours at least. It was dusk. A golden light seeped into the room. What would normally be a romantic, heart-lifting splash of color had transformed into something out of the most depraved nightmare.

He hovered over the bed holding the dagger. With one fluid motion, he slit her shirt open from neck to waist. Using the blade, he flicked the scraps of fabric back off her chest and then sliced through the band of her bra. It snapped to the sides, and her breasts popped out. His lips were wet in the slit revealing his mouth, and he sucked in air sharply at the sight.

"Do it." Her words were slurred from the drug. "Kill me."

He lifted his head slightly so his eyes were on her face. Then, barely perceptible, he slowly shook his head.

Putting the dagger's handle in his mouth, he climbed on top of her and reached down and yanked her pants down to her knees where they got stuck on her boots. She tried to squirm out from under him, but her muscles weren't receiving the signal yet. "No!" she screamed.

He cut her leggings off in pieces, leaving her naked with her boots still on.

He rose back to straddle her hips and held the knife to her throat. She tried in vain to thrust her neck into the blade, but he easily jerked the knife back. The drug had dulled her reflexes and made it nearly impossible to even move. She paused. He wanted her alive. Well then... she would do everything in her power to die before it happened.

He could have his way with a corpse.

Starting at her collarbone, he drew the blade quickly and lightly down her chest. She felt warm, sticky blood ooze from a shallow cut.

"Kill me." She hissed the words. They were less slurred. The drug was wearing off. She found she could flex her ankle and did so gingerly, hoping he wouldn't notice that she was regaining her ability to move.

She watched and waited until he dipped his head in concentration, bringing his head within range. She jerked her head smacking it into his nose, but it was weak, ineffective. He grabbed a hunk of her hair, yanking it so fiercely she howled in pain and when he drew back, he was holding a clump of her hair.

She flailed and jerked. He reached over to the bedside table, and a second later she felt another needle jab in her neck. Her slight ability to move seeped instantly away.

But this time she didn't pass out. She watched as he took the blade to her again, making small marks across her abdomen. He was slowly and methodically torturing her.

He took a smaller blade and stabbed her. A jab here and there. Although his face was masked, she could sense his glee. Over and over, he slipped the blade into her naked flesh but not deep enough to kill. She knew the pain would come. But right now, all was numb. Her head was clear but her body paralyzed.

He sometimes held the blade aloft so she could see her blood dripping from it.

"I will leave you alive, but I will make sure you never forget my visit." It was the first time he had spoken. The Sicilian words fell out of his mouth. Why was his voice familiar?

Her mind went on high alert. She tried to respond, but her mouth was useless. Instead, a small bit of drool formed in the corner of her lip. His voice was familiar. Her mind raced, trying to identify the dialect. Was it her own?

Again and again, she tried to move, waiting for the drug to wear off, but nothing happened. Her limbs remained useless.

The only way she knew she was crying was that her vision had grown blurry, as if she were underwater. The tears pooled in her eyes before overflowing down her cheeks. She decided to close her eyes and act like she'd passed out or was sleeping. She wanted him to feel secure that she was no longer a threat. That way when the drug wore off, she could attack.

After a while, he left her side and sat in the gold and green Victorian upholstered chair in the corner—the one she'd curl up in while she read. His legs were splayed out before him. He reached over to her dresser and took a sip of something out of a bottle.

Eva watched him through slitted eyes.

But she breathed loudly and even tried to make it sound like she was snoring. She couldn't tell for sure, but it seemed like his head had tilted slightly to the side, as if he might have dozed off, as well. Good.

The first indication that feeling was returning was an intense, searing, white-hot pain that dotted and sparked across her chest. All the stab wounds. The pain was excruciating. Slowly so he wouldn't notice, she tried to flex her toes and fingers. Her ability to move was returning. She concentrated. She needed to channel that pain into pure rage. That would be the only thing that might save her. Soon, soon, she'd be able to move, and he would pay.

After a few minutes, he leaped up and raced over to the bed. Inwardly, she braced for a blow from the dagger that would end her life, but instead he reached down to her wrist and felt her pulse. It must have been weak because it seemingly worried him enough to press his head to her chest. She considered grabbing him and breaking his neck right then and there, but although she could move, her reflexes were probably still slower than usual, and her strength might be zapped. It was too dangerous. By the time he realized she could move again, she needed to be halfway out the door.

Because right then, with her body bleeding out and her limbs so shaky and numb, she wasn't confident she'd be able to stand up, let alone kill that son of a bitch.

Seemingly satisfied that she was breathing, he lifted his head and scooted off the bed, peeling the rubber suit off and stepping out of it completely, leaving the rubber mask on. She watched him through her eyelashes. He flicked the bathroom light on, filling some of the bedroom with a dim light. The bed where she lay remained in shadow. He cast a glance back at the bed as he stood in front of the mirror above the dresser naked, his taut buttocks facing her. She watched and waited. Then he peeled off the rubber mask. It took everything she had to stifle her gasp.

It was Nikos. From the school.

He was not Greek. He was Sicilian. He'd only come to the school a year ago. That meant he'd lain in wait to torture her for an entire year.

His eyes flickered over to the bed again and she squeezed her eyes shut tight. She could hear his footsteps padding toward the bathroom. Her blood pounded with excitement. Her muscles tensed, ready for flight. She heard him turn on the shower.

Once he was in the shower, she could dart in and attack him before he even realized what was happening. Right now, with her wounds, she needed every advantage she could find. Her body tensed, waiting in anticipation.

He stood naked in front of the shower door as steam started to pour into the room. She started to lift her head but froze when he glanced back into the room. She knew the sound of the water would muffle her movements, so as soon as he stepped toward the shower, she leaned forward, reaching deep into her boot. She drew out the dagger. As her hand reached inside her boot, she felt her cell phone.

She punched in Detective Collin's number and threw the phone on the bed before rushing toward the bathroom.

Holding the dagger before her, she saw the empty shower at the same time she felt the kick to her kidney. She collapsed onto the floor, turning as she fell to thrust the dagger toward him. She sliced Nikos's thigh, drawing blood and a scream of anguish. Blood began to gush, and she scrambled on all fours back toward the bedroom. She was nearly to the bed and phone when a hand twisted in her hair and yanked her head back. Nikos stood over her, naked, holding her gun.

His face was red, his chest heaving. Blood oozed out from the towel he'd tied around his leg. He looked down at her, his face twisted in a mask of fury. She heard a click as he undid the safety on the gun. She stared back at him, defiantly. She would die with honor.

They both heard a voice in the room, a tinny sound from far away. Detective Collins.

Nikos eyes flicked to the phone on the bed. It seemed to snap him back.

"If it were up to me, you would have died the first moment I saw you."

She smiled.

He frowned. "What's so funny."

"Up to you? So, you're not in charge? You think you're a stone-cold killer, but you're really just someone's bitch."

He kicked her in the ribs, sending her back to the floor groaning and gasping in pain. At the same time, she heard shouting from the phone. When she sat up again, he was gone. She heard the sound of his footsteps racing down the stairs. The pile of clothes he'd discarded outside the bathroom door was gone.

As she scrambled to her feet, she heard a motorcycle roar away.

That's why she hadn't seen a car. She still couldn't figure out how he'd gained entry to the house without leaving a trace. Unless. Unless he had come in the same way she had.

It suddenly dawned on her that the police probably hadn't found the secret room, but he had. He'd probably arrived just moments before her, leaving the door wide open as a trap. He may have even been hiding outside, waiting for her to enter first and search it so she would feel safe and let her guard down—just as she had done— before his attack.

All this raced through her head as she stumbled to the bathroom, using the wall to support herself. She left bloody handprints on everything she touched. Like the rest of the house, the bathroom was trashed—the contents of the medicine cabinet had been dumped on the floor. She kneeled and frantically sorted through the assorted bottles and containers until she found the painkillers. She grabbed a dress out of a pile on the floor and pulled it on over her bare body, then slipped inside the secret room and closed the door behind her.

It was only once she was down the staircase and under the deck that she remembered her burner cell left on the bed with the line open to the detective. For once, she regretted making the burner phone untraceable. But then, to her surprise, she heard the distant whine of sirens. Maybe the detective was smarter than she thought and had put together the same clues as she had. It had just taken him a lot longer.

Eva felt like she was going to vomit as she stumbled down the beach. She'd planned to get to her car, using the cover of night, but realized that her wounds were too great. She needed to rest and maybe get stitches. She turned toward the Camden's house. Once inside, she quickly glanced at a laminated sheet on the counter. It gave instructions for the house and its care while the owners were gone. She'd seen it earlier. Now she scanned for dates.

The maid wouldn't come for another week. Thank God. She yanked open a cupboard and grabbed the first food she saw—two cans of peaches with a pull tab, a box of crackers, and four tins of sardines. Clutching these provisions, she made her way up to the second-floor bathroom where she could see her house. She propped herself up against the wall and watched as a convoy of police cars and ambulances pulled into her driveway. Cops emerged from their vehicles, guns drawn, and raced toward the house.

Good old Collins. Did this mean he believed her now?

She stripped and stepped into the shower without turning on the bathroom lights. Glancing down as the blood washed off her and formed a pool of frothy pink on the shower floor, she tried to examine her wounds. Most seemed shallow. One, low on her abdomen, gaped open. She needed to do something to stem the blood flow. But first she wanted to clean them. When she lathered soap into her wounds, she collapsed onto the shower floor, nearly passing out from the pain.

She tried to stand and slumped back down onto the shower floor. Hard. It took all of her effort to reach one hand outside the shower and rummage in her boot for the bottle of painkillers. She tossed a handful of them in her mouth and then opened her mouth like a baby bird capturing some of the warm water beating down so she could swallow them. She rested one hand on the shower wall and moaned, praying the painkillers would work before the hot water ran out. She needed something to fight the pain so she could crawl into the guest bedroom and sleep.

Finally, after what seemed like forever, the pain seemed to lessen. She tried to stand and, this time, managed to stay up. She turned the faucet off and wrapped herself in one of the huge plush towels hanging from a towel rack. Dripping pink, blood-stained water behind her, she peeked into the master bedroom's medicine cabinet and found some bandages.

She emptied the box. And the blood was still seeping through. She realized she'd need something more. Down in the garage on a small shelf she found some super glue. She sterilized her wounds with some rubbing alcohol and then after drying her skin, used the super glue to seal her deepest cuts.

Back upstairs again, exhausted from her efforts, she found a soft, navy blue velour tracksuit that was a few sizes too big. Thank you, Mrs. Camden. She managed to put the tracksuit on and made her way into the guest bedroom where she pulled back the covers on the bed and crawled inside.

Soon, she was drifting off to sleep. But she kept jerking back awake in excruciating pain. She'd stopped the external bleeding, but maybe she was bleeding internally. Had he lacerated her liver? Could you bleed out from that? Most of the cuts seemed shallow, but who knew? The pain didn't feel like it was shallow, that's for sure. Maybe she was going to die. Guilt swarmed through her.

She wished she had the energy to write a note to Mr. and Mrs. Camden, telling them she was sorry for breaking into their home. If she made it out of their house alive, she'd anonymously send them a substantial amount of cash to make up for it. But right then, she wasn't sure she would make it out of the house alive. She shook off that thought. She had to survive. She had to heal. Because before she succumbed to death, she needed to hunt down Nikos and make him pay in a way he'd never imagined, even in his worst nightmares.

19

Los Angeles

A week later, she knew she'd survive. She'd gone through three days of fevers, which she was sure stemmed from infected wounds. Feverish and nearly delirious, on the second day of the fever, she'd managed to make her way to the master bath medicine cabinet and found some antibiotics. They had expired two months before, but they seemed to do the trick because on the fourth day she'd woken up clearheaded again. She'd found a case of bottled water under the sink in the master bath and had dragged it back into the guest room with her, putting it beside her in bed. She knew that she could do without food, but water was another issue.

Ravenous, she'd scarfed down peaches and sardines, but now that her fever had broken, she knew she'd never eat either food again.

The first day she woke without a fever, she got out of bed and gingerly did some stretching and mild strength training. She couldn't afford to lose the strength she'd built up over the years. At first, it involved curls with canned peaches, but before long she was able to do some very, very gentle crunches and push-ups. She was careful not to open her wounds, but even so, one day she had to super glue a larger cut that opened during her stretching.

Each day, she worked out, considering it physical therapy. Each workout left her exhausted and sweating and dizzy, but she pushed herself a little more each day.

On the sixth day, she remembered the maid was scheduled to come so she woke early, scrubbed the bathroom, cleaned up her mess, and made the bed in the guest room. Then she spent the entire day hidden in a basement storage room that she barricaded from the inside. The maid didn't show up until noon. As she heard the sounds of vacuuming and banging around above her, Eva remained in the dank, dark space until she heard the maid leave.

She sank into the guest bed with relief, knowing she had the house to herself for another week. The next week, she hid from the maid again. After the maid left, Eva cleaned the guest room and bathroom that she'd used and then stepped into the garage with a wad of keys she'd seen hanging on a hook in the entry way. She left the Hummer and, instead, stepped into the Volvo station wagon. She knew the car wouldn't be reported stolen for at least another week when the maid returned.

Back at her new house, she threw open the windows to let in fresh air and unearthed one of her burner phones. She dialed Detective Collins.

"You're alive." He spoke before she did. "With the amount of blood we found at your house, I thought maybe you were a goner."

She grunted in reply, wondering how he knew it was her on the other end of the line.

"I don't give this number out to just anyone," he said, reading her mind.

"Only the girls you really care about?"

"Exactly," he said. He sounded happy she'd called.

"I haven't watched the news. Am I still a suspect?" He paused.

"Guess that's a yes."

"I haven't made up my mind."

"Listen. The killer? He was the one who stabbed me nearly to death. And I know who it is now. That's why I'm calling."

106KRISTI BELCAMINO

"It's a man now?"

"Nikos Alexopoulos."

"Is that name supposed to mean something to me?"

"He was the father of one of my children's classmates." Silence.

"He withdrew his kid from school shortly after the...deaths." It pained her to say the word.

"I'll check into it."

"It would be a lot easier for me to find him if you lifted this arrest warrant off my head."

"Not gonna happen."

"Even if you prove he did it?"

"Even if."

"Did you find the wig and mask in my house?"

"Actually, we did."

Eva sighed audibly with relief. "Do you believe me now?"

"I wanted to try it on," he continued, "to see if I would look like you, but the forensic tech guys didn't want me to touch it. They sent it away to see if they can extract DNA."

"So I'm cleared, right? No more arrest warrant?"

"Oh, there is still an arrest warrant."

"What?"

"You're forgetting one key detail." She waited.

"You killed a man right in front of a witness."

She actually had forgotten that part. Krystal. "You mean because I saved a woman's life and she doesn't understand that."

"A jury will determine whether it was self-defense."

"I didn't say it was self-defense," Eva said, her jaw tightening. "I said I saved a woman's life. What is wrong with your country?"

This time the detective was silent. As soon as she said it, she knew she'd made a major mistake. She'd let him know that she wasn't an American-born citizen.

But he seemed to brush it off, saying, "That's all fine and good if it's true, but it would still be up to a jury to decide that, and I'm sorry to say, but putting your sole eyewitness up on the stand isn't going to help your case."

He paused. She remained quiet. She had nothing to say to that.

He continued, "Why does she hate you so much?"

"Any number of reasons, I guess," she glanced at the time. "Hey, when I called how did you know I was calling from my old house?"

"Somebody called it in."

"What in?"

"Some old guy saw you walking down the beach from the parking lot."

Eva thought about that for a second. "That was about an hour before I was inside my house."

"I didn't get the tip until right before you called me. I put two and two together."

For a second, she almost thanked him, but instead she hung up and tossed the phone across the room. They weren't friends. He was the enemy. She wasn't sure why she'd called him for help anyway.

She didn't need his help. She didn't need him at all. What she needed was to find Nikos and make him pay. Meanwhile, she would start preparing for battle.

She dug out some leggings and a sports bra, laced up her running shoes, and began her training. Four hours. Then a break. And then four hours more.

Her recovery was over. Even though her wounds still ached and threatened to split open, she was done lying around in bed. It was time to start warrior training. She wanted to be in top shape for battle. Now that she knew the face of her enemy, nothing would stop her.

20

Los Angeles

Late that night, sitting in the light from her laptop, Eva began her Dark Web search for Nikos Alexopoulos.

But then she paused. Might as well search the easy stuff first. She hacked into the school's website and files and pulled up the information on Nikos Alexopoulos and his son's registration.

Not surprisingly, when she pulled up the address on Google satellite, she saw it belonged to a strip mall mailing center in Cerritos.

When she searched for the address itself, she came across something interesting. It was registered to a Vincenzo Scannacristiana. Was that Nikos' real name?

The surname meant "People Slayer" in Sicilian dialect. He was an assassin of the highest order. She'd heard that the name was passed down from generation to generation, and only one person could hold the title in a lifetime.

He basically held the title of King of the Assassins in Sicily. And he was after her.

Eva searched the Italian newspapers and websites for information on the latest incarnation of this generation's lo scannacristiana. A blurry photo taken from surveillance footage at a funeral four years before revealed a photo showing the man's face, but only in profile. Eva enlarged it and then gaped. It was unmistakable. Vincenzo Scannacristiana was Nikos Alexopoulos. But there was more.

In the photo, he was dipping his head about to duck into the backseat of a livery car. Eva zoomed in on the picture. Inside the car, already seated, was a frail-looking older woman in a black dress, gloves, and veil. Eva's heart pounded. They were attending a funeral. She clicked on the photo to get to the article.

Vincenzo was attending his uncle's—Alberto Cannuci's—funeral.

Eva's mouth grew dry. No wonder she'd always been so drawn to Nikos and felt like he was a kindred spirit. He was her childhood friend—Vincenzo Canucci.

She'd last seen him in Sicily when they were both ten. Their parents had been close friends. They spent Sunday suppers and even some holidays together. Her best friend, Tomas, always felt left out because even though he was Eva's best friend, his parents were not in her parents' inner circle. To be in that inner circle you had to be a Mafioso.

But the year Eva turned ten, her father suddenly grew cold when it came to the Canucci family. They were no longer invited over for supper or for outings to Sardinia or other holidays. And worst of all, her father forbade her from playing with Vincenzo. Within a month, the Canucci family had disappeared.

Eva discovered this one Saturday when her mother sent her on an errand into town to buy eggs. She took a detour that led her right in front of the Canucci's small two-story house perched on a hill. She'd hoped that Vincenzo would be looking out the window as she passed, and maybe he'd smile at her. She knew better than to go knock on the door or initiate conversation in any way. Her father's temper was not to be trifled with.

But as she side-eyed the house, she noticed the front door was wide open, and the house was empty. She ran over to it and glanced inside. There was nothing there. Not even one tiny piece of furniture. It was unheard of in her life.

In Sicily, even if people moved for some reason, they left their furniture behind, and somebody else stayed in the house until they could return or until a family member could move in. Nobody bought and sold property in those years. Instead, homes were kept in families for generations, passed down for eternity. At least in those days.

Eva's shock could not have been greater. Tears sprung to her eyes.

She forgot about the eggs and ran home. She flung open the front door and, instead of knocking as required, she burst into her father's study, startling a group of men who stood there.

Her father's eyes narrowed, and his face grew red. She immediately knew she'd made a grievous mistake.

"Sorry." She backed out of the room, heart pounding.

She immediately ran into the nearby bathroom, grabbing the water glass and pressing it to the wall so she could eavesdrop. It was something she'd read in a detective story.

To her surprise, it worked.

"My apologies. She is a strong-willed child. I will teach her manners later."

Upon hearing this, Eva trembled in fear.

She kept listening even though the glass pressed up against her ear was starting to be painful.

"They will no longer cause us problems," her father said.

"Are you certain?"

"Do you question me?" Her father's tone was calm and dangerous.

"No. No, of course not."

"Good."

She heard a chair scrape against the floor. "If there is nothing else, I must attend to my daughter and teach her some manners."

Eva didn't wait to hear the rest. She tore out of the bathroom and then through the front door, running all the way into town. When she returned home later, her father was not home.

The next morning, she pretended to be busy in her room until it was time to walk to church. She stayed close to her mother, holding the woman's hand while her two brothers walked ahead with her father.

Sitting in the pew at mass, she prayed fervently that her father would go easy on her. And it worked. He never mentioned her barging into his study. And she never mentioned the Canucci family.

Vincenzo Canucci was now the People Slayer. And he was after her.

The Mafia had sent their top assassin—her childhood friend—to kill her family.

She read more about the People Slayer, stunned that a boy who had been too sweet to step on a spider, had become a cold-blooded killer. The article talked about how ruthless lo scannacristiana was. How he had kidnapped the son of a rival and held the child captive for a year. Even though the father turned himself in, begging for mercy, Cannuci had still killed the child in front of his father before letting him go, to live with his grief. Then, lo scannacristiana had performed lupara bianca. It was a final slap in the face. The term meant that he had either destroyed or hidden the child's body, so the family could not honor him or mourn at a funeral mass.

As soon as Eva read that, she panicked. Had they held a funeral mass for her family while she was delirious and recovering from her injuries?

After forcing herself to calm down and do some deep breathing, she was able to search online for notice of a burial or services for her family. She knew that the public's interest in her family's slayings meant it would have made the news.

She didn't find anything and sat back in relief.

Although she hated to do it, she picked up the phone and dialed Collins.

"One more thing. What about funeral arrangements for my family?"

She kept her voice cold, neutral.

"Some family members from Washington state have been in touch. They are asking permission to take the bodies there for burial."

Eva closed her eyes. Even though it would break her heart not to be there, it was for the best.

She hung up without replying.

21

Sicily

"You don't deserve your name."

The voice on the phone was full of venom. Vincenzo bowed his head in shame. The waves thundered outside the door of his trailer on the strip of beach north of Laguna Seca. Somewhere, thirty miles north, Eva Lucia Santella still lived.

But then his pride took over. He knew The Arm was playing a power game by remaining silent, willing him to speak first, but he didn't care, it must be said.

"You are not allowing me to do as my name requires."

For a second, Vincenzo wondered if the words were a fatal mistake. Not very many people argued with Luigi the Arm. Had he just signed his own death warrant? It most likely depended on whether anyone else was in the room with The Arm. If he were on speaker phone, he might be killed just to set an example. A lesson about how anybody, even his most treasured assassin and surrogate son, would die for speaking disrespectfully to Luigi the Arm.

"As the lo scannacristiana, your charge is to follow orders. You are not necessarily going to be privy to the final plans. You know that."

"I was out of line."

"You want this as badly as me. This is what we've waited years for, son."

"Yes, I know." But you want her alive, and I want her dead. "My apologies."

The hard-won words were greeted by a chilly silence.

He cleared his throat. "My anger on your behalf fills me with blood thirst," he said. "I simply want to avenge you and yours. I, of course, will always trust your judgement and do as you say. My loyalty is to you and your desires, not my own. To the death." He wondered if the old man was convinced.

The Arm exhaled loudly into the phone. "Yes. I know this. I know that you want revenge as much as I do. That is our bond, my son. Just continue as I've directed."

"Yes, sir."

"And Vincenzo?"

"Yes?"

"Know this—you will get your chance. This vendetta is almost as much yours as it is mine."

When the line disconnected, Vincenzo was overcome with emotion. He would be allowed to take her life. He could do it and return a hero to his homeland. Because ever since he was an adolescent, Vincenzo's only desire in life was to make the Santella family pay. And despite The Arm's belief that Eva living with her guilt was the best punishment, Nikos knew much, much better forms of punishment. She'd only just got a taste of what he had in mind. He'd only been taking a quick break when she'd escaped. He'd made a critical mistake, assuming because of her body weight that she wouldn't take much of the drug to be immobilized. Vincenzo only made mistakes once.

Thinking about this in the beach trailer gave him an enormous erection. Imagining how he would make a member of the Santella family pay was the greatest turn-on in his life. Standing against the sliding glass window he began to pleasure himself, watching the people frolicking on the beach only twenty yards away. It wasn't the first time he'd done this. A year away from his wife and mistress was a very long time for a man filled with the lustful yearnings he had. And torturing Eva Santella had made him extraordinarily horny.

His eyes slit in pleasure as he thought of his mistress back home —Henrietta. The only woman his wife allowed him to dally with, although it was never openly acknowledged or spoken about. His wife turned the other cheek because she knew very well that Henrietta would do things she wouldn't do, and frankly, things he didn't feel comfortable doing to the mother of his children.

He continued to stroke himself, watching the passerby. If one of them happened to glance over, they wouldn't be able to see him standing in the shadowy trailer, but he imagined they could as he stroked himself. His eyes lost focus, and he came loudly and violently, his entire body convulsing as he let out a powerful half moan, half scream.

22

Los Angeles

Eva double-checked the address.

This was most definitely the house.

Eva had spent the past three days staking out the post office box location. It was only this morning, around seven that she finally saw a woman enter the strip mall post office and head toward the corner box. She wore scrubs. Her hair was teased to twice its size, and her eyes were thickly lined with black kohl. She looked to be in her mid-twenties. She glanced around furtively before she stuck the key in the box.

It must have been empty, because even from her car, Eva could see the woman's mouth utter an expletive as she slammed the box shut and then kicked a row of boxes below.

Obviously, the mail she was expecting had not arrived.

The woman left on foot, and Eva tailed her to this small home in a rundown Cerritos neighborhood.

Rusted and beat-up cars had taken over what once had been front lawns. Every door and window had metal bars. The few homes with fences had locked gates and barbed wire trailing along the tops.

The house she was parked in front of had a small front porch and a dirt yard covered with toys. A driveway led to a small garage in the back.

Inside the open door was a shiny, blue SUV with dealer's plates on it. Eva watched the woman go in through the front door. A few minutes later, she emerged from the side yard, trailing after a small boy in a striped T-shirt and diaper who was wandering toward the street.

The boy's face was dirty and tear streaked.

"Ricardo! It's time to leave for school! Help me get your brother!"

A boy came out of the house, shrugging a backpack onto one shoulder.

It was Ricardo. He had what looked like dark shadows under his eyes. But then Eva realized there was a faded bruise under one eye.

Ricardo scooped up the younger boy in a bear hug and started toward the garage in the back. The woman went back in the front door and then emerged dangling car keys and a large diaper bag. She locked the door behind her, glancing at the street. For a second she met Eva's eyes. Eva held her gaze for an instant, but the woman quickly looked down and hurried to the garage.

It wasn't ideal, but Eva needed answers. She pulled the Volvo across the driveway, blocking the path of the blue SUV as it began to back out. Leaving the car running, Eva got out and leaned against her hood with her arms crossed until the woman stopped her vehicle.

She waited.

Finally, the woman got out of her vehicle and walked over. "What do you want? I'm late for work, and my son's going to be late for school."

"Your son? How much did he pay you?"

"What?"

"To pretend that Ricardo was his adopted son."

"None of your goddamn business."

"Enough to buy that car?" Eva's voice was even. "Also enough to help pay the rent and buy food I hope."

"We're not a charity case," the woman said, her eyes narrowing. "I have a good job."

"I DIDN'T SAY you didn't. I just figured it must have been a lot for you to let him take your son."

"Mama! Mama! Mama!" The small voice came from the back seat of the

SUV. The baby was crying. Ricardo pulled the child out of its car seat and hugged him, trying to soothe the boy.

An older woman walking by in a house dress with a walker paused on the sidewalk between Eva and Ricardo's mother.

"Everything okay here?" she asked the young mother, ignoring Eva.

"Yes, Mrs. Gonzales. Thank you."

The gray-haired woman nodded and continued on without looking Eva's way.

"You seem like you've got nice neighbors here. People who look out for one another."

"Yes?" The woman narrowed her eyes suspiciously.

"Mrs. White?" Ricardo had finally turned and noticed what was going on behind him.

"Be right there, Ricardo," the woman said.

"How is he?" Eva's voice was soft.

The woman scoffed. "What do you think? He got yanked out of his big fancy school, and now he's at Washington Central. It's a breeding ground for criminals. He came home with a black eye yesterday. You happy about that?"

"You seem to think this is my fault." Eva's kept her words neutral and measured.

"It is," the woman said. "Ricardo was doing so good in that school. That's all I wanted for him. I wanted the same opportunity that your children had. But you've taken that away. His new school? Besides the black eye, do you know what happened last week? His classmate brought a gun to school. A nine-year-old. It's your fault. And you should get the hell away from me before I call the police. You're psycho. What kind of mother kills her children?"

Eva remained expressionless. The woman said it as if murder were normal. Maybe in this neighborhood it was. The only thing that seemed to bother her was that Eva had killed her children, not that Eva had killed.

"We're almost done here," Eva said. "One last question. Did Nikos pick Ricardo up every day or did Ricardo live with him, as well?"

The woman's eyes widened. "Ricardo lived here, of course. Nikos just picked him up and dropped him off." Eva nodded.

"Give me his contact information. The number where you reached him."

The woman's face crinkled. "Why would I do that?" "Nikos is the one who killed my family." The woman's forehead creased.

Eva met her gaze with a steely expression. The woman stared and then blinked and nodded. She believed her. She must have sensed that the man she knew as Nikos was capable of such things. Ricardo's mother reached for a cell phone in her pocket. Withdrawing it, she tapped on the screen and then held it up to Eva's face. Eva memorized the number. She turned to get back in her car but then paused and turned back to the woman, who was still standing there scowling, hands on her hips.

"I have a good job, you know," the woman said, squaring her shoulders. "I work in a clinic. But it's not enough. My husband is in prison. For life. So I'm on my own. With two kids. All my money goes to Enrico's preschool."

Eva nodded hoping the gesture conveyed respect for this proud, hard-working, single mother.

"If Ricardo and your younger son's tuition was paid for, would you be able to get them to the academy every day? Would your job allow that?"

The woman gaped, her mouth wide open. Eva tilted her head, waiting.

Then the woman seemed to realize what Eva was saying. "Yes. Yes. I could drive them. Enrico is only two, though. He wouldn't be able to go to their preschool program until next month when he turns three."

The school was preschool through eighth grade. Most students then went on to private high schools. Eva didn't know if she would be alive tomorrow, much less nine years from now, so it would have to be enough to cover both boys through eighth grade.

"Consider it done," Eva said.

"How do I know what you're saying is true. What if I show up at the school and they turn us away? I'm not going to do that to Ricardo. He's embarrassed enough that he had to leave there."

"It will be arranged by Monday."

Eva turned and got into her car. She pulled out of the SUV's way and parked, dipping her head to make the financial arrangements and money transfer on her phone before she dialed the school with a burner phone.

Adopting a slightly British accent, she told the school secretary that an anonymous donor was sending the school a wire transfer to pay for Ricardo and his brother to attend the academy through eighth grade.

23

When she pulled up to her gate, she saw a bright blur of color moving quickly from the bushes. She reached for her gun and had it pointed at the window in time to see Dolan's face blanch in horror.

He careened back, tripping and falling onto the pavement.

She hopped out to help him up. "I'm so sorry." Seeing him again sent another shock of grief through her. She knew he and Lorenzo would've been fast friends. She could almost imagine the two of them riding their bikes together up and down this road. She pushed away those thoughts and apologized again. "You okay?"

He shook his head. "I thought you were going to shoot me."

"You have to be careful about scaring people like that," she said.

"Yeah. I forgot that cops always have guns."

Guilt flooded her, but she had to keep letting him believe she was a police officer. It was the only way to explain stupid things like her pointing a gun at his face. Twice.

"What's up?" she said once she'd helped him up and put his bike on its kickstand. He brushed himself off, his face slightly red. She was slightly irritated. She was in a hurry to get inside her place and track the phone number Ricardo's mother had given her for Nikos.

"Remember that thing I told you?'

"About your dad?"

"Yeah." He looked down and prodded one scuffed tennis shoe into the pavement. She couldn't see his eyes. The brim of his baseball cap hid most of his face.

"What's going on now?"

"He's in the hospital. He had to have surgery. But I'm scared. I don't know if he's going to come home. I don't want to go live with my mom."

"Who is at the house with you?"

"My stepdad. Well, my dad's husband."

Every fiber of her being was telling her to get rid of the kid so she could rush inside and track down Nikos, but when she saw the boy's face, she knew she had to help.

"Do you want to do that DNA test now?" Her voice was soft, but matter of fact.

He looked up and nodded eagerly.

"Okay," she said.

"Okay?"

"Yes. I picked one up yesterday. Why don't you come up to the house with me, and we'll submit it?"

"Right now?"

"Yes."

He set his bike inside the gate and hopped into the passenger seat.

For a second, Eva hesitated. She was bringing someone else into her secret hideout. The kid would probably think it odd that all the living room furniture had been pushed into a spare bedroom. The living room was now outfitted as a training room and gym. But when Dolan stepped inside, he grinned and ran over to heft up the ten-pound weights.

"This is so cool. You don't even have a couch. Just a gym. Are all cop's houses like this?"

"I don't know," she answered honestly.

She pulled out a bar stool at the kitchen counter and patted it. "Come sit here. Let's get the test ready."

Pulling it out of the paper bag, she read the instructions. "Okay, seems simple enough. But you should know we have to mail it in and it could take as long as a month to get the results."

Dolan frowned but said, "That's okay."

She swabbed the inside of his cheek, sealed the container and set it on the counter.

She watched from a window as Dolan walked down the driveway. She opened the gates remotely, and after he headed up the hill with his bike, she closed them again.

Poor kid. She hoped his biological father wasn't a scum bag. If so, she would never tell him. The mother couldn't be that bad, could she? Eva decided to find out.

The mother was that bad.

It hadn't taken very long for Eva to pull up more information than she ever wanted to know about Miranda Edwards. The mother was a child psychologist—go figure—and from her website photo, she looked like a ball breaker. Deeper digging into the sealed divorce and custody court records revealed that Miranda had abused Dolan. She'd locked him in a closet for twelve hours and said he was just like his father—a coward and probably gay. Eva tried to contain her rage and keep her head as she read more. The woman was a monster. And she was not only messing up her own son, she was messing up other people's children. Eva read on.

It got worse. There was an accusation of sexual abuse—that Miranda Edwards had forced Dolan to watch her have sex with a construction worker when he was four years old. Dolan's father apparently walked in on it. After beating the crap out of the man and slapping his wife across the face, he was the one who was arrested. Despite visits from child protective services, the judge still agreed to joint custody based on that arrest.

When questioned, Dolan didn't remember the incident. A psychiatrist testified that the boy had disassociated and blocked it from his memory.

Eva balled her fists. Fury coursed through her. This woman did not deserve her son. She deserved to be shot. Eva closed her eyes. God willing, the father would survive his illness because if he died and left his son to live with that psychopath it would be either a death sentence or a one-way ticket to hell for the kid.

Miranda Edwards would not get custody of Dolan if it was the last thing Eva did.

Eva dug around more. She hacked her way into a work computer. From there, it was fairly simple to access her personal email account.

There she found photos of the woman having sex with a teenage boy in her office. Eva would bet the boy wasn't eighteen and was probably a patient. That alone was enough for Eva to quickly print them out. It was exactly the ammunition she needed. Her job was to make sure the father and stepfather got full custody of the boy—and that the mother never saw Dolan again.

Eva then logged onto the Dark Web and paid for another hacker to access the "find my phone" feature for Vincenzo's cell phone. She was counting on him not being as cautious as she was about his cell phone being traced. Within the hour, she had the results.

The phone pinged in Laguna Beach. She pulled the location up on Maps and then zoomed in on the satellite image. It grew dark and Eva made plans to rise early to go visit Dolan's mother. As much as she wanted to go after Vincenzo then and there, Eva had made a promise to herself. She would make sure Dolan never had to live with his mother.

Vincenzo would have to wait. She paid the hacker extra to notify her immediately if the phone left the Laguna Beach location.

The next morning, Eva dressed in black leather pants, knee-high boots, and a black long-sleeve top. She slicked on red lipstick and donned huge, black sunglasses. Before 6:00 a.m., she strode in the front door of the woman's Beverly Hills house after picking the lock. Her gun was tucked into a shoulder holster and clearly visible.

Miranda was seated at the counter in her kitchen sipping on a fruit smoothie and looking at her phone. When Eva stalked in, she damn near fell backward off the bar stool, swearing. "Jesus Christ!

Who are you? Edgar!"

A man in a white shirt and black pants—clearly the help—ran into the kitchen.

He pulled up short when Eva met his eyes and tapped the gun in its holster.

"Calm down," she said. "I just want to talk."

"Get the hell out of my house," Miranda said, backing up against the refrigerator.

"Sit down," Eva ordered. Miranda glared at her, but she sat back down, this time at the kitchen table. Eva turned to the man. "You too." He slid into a seat next to Miranda.

Eva threw a stapled set of documents and a manila envelope down on the glass table and folded her arms across her chest. "Sign that document. You are agreeing to give up all custody and any visitation rights regarding Dolan."

"Jonathan is not even his father!"

"Sign the goddamn papers, now."

Miranda laughed—a panicked, high tinkling sound—and glanced at her companion. "Edgar, would you call the police please?"

The man squirmed uncomfortably. "Um."

"Wait." Eva's voice was calm, but she held out her palm toward the man. He froze. Then she turned toward Dolan's mother. "Before you do that, I think you should look at what's inside the envelope."

The woman's careful façade cracked slightly. Eva saw fear shoot across her face. She reached down and gingerly picked up the envelope. She turned her back to them and slid the photos out. Eva watched the woman's back heave violently when she saw the photos.

Miranda turned to Eva, her face expressionless.

"Where do I sign?"

Eva scooped up the signed document, leaving the envelope with photos on the table.

"Keep those. They're a reminder to you of what will happen if I ever hear that you've contacted Dolan. Ever."

Eva turned and walked out.

HER NEXT STOP was the hospital.

Before getting out of the Camden's Volvo, she pulled her hair into a ponytail and tucked it into a baseball cap, which she pulled down to her eyes. She shrugged on a beat-up Army jacket. She watched through the window in the door for a moment.

Dolan's father had Elvis Costello glasses and the same lock of hair falling into his eyes as his son, but his hair was black. He looked like he was in his forties. His wiry build reminded Eva of a marathon runner.

He looked up in surprise when she walked in. Then his eyes narrowed when he saw her holding the stapled documents. "Did my ex-wife send you?"

Eva laughed. "Not exactly. But I do have something from her."

She handed him the papers. He took them, glowering, and pulled himself upright to read them. She watched as his eyes widened, and the blood drained from his face.

"Who are you?" he said looking up. His hand was shaking.

"I'm your new neighbor."

His forehead crinkled. "You're the cop who bought the Hinkley house?"

Eva didn't want to lie so she said, "If the Hinkley house is the one right below yours, then yes." She gestured to a chair. "Do you mind?" "No, sorry, please sit."

Eva sat down and smiled. "I met Dolan shortly after I moved in. He mentioned you were ill and that he was worried about having to go live with his mother."

"He did?" The man looked pained.

"He also said how much he liked your husband and wanted to stay with him...while you were recovering," Eva lied smoothly.

He gave a small smile when Eva mentioned his husband.

"But I don't understand," he said. "She would never sign this willingly. She told me once she'd rather die than give me what I wanted. She doesn't care about Dolan. She's poison. I spend every day trying to counteract her abuse. I'll never forgive myself for being so blind. I was so worried about myself and what coming out would mean for my son that I didn't see what was right in front of me."

"Don't beat yourself up for another second," Eva said. "Your son seems very well adjusted and thinks the world of you and your husband. I think he has a very good life ahead of him."

"It kills me that she still gets to see him. It's supervised custody when he's over there, but still. She is pure venom."

Eva stood and looked pointedly at the papers. "Well," she said, "you don't have to worry about that anymore. You can concentrate on healing and getting back home to Dolan and your husband." He closed his eyes. His hands had curled into fists.

His eyes opened. "But what if I don't? Get better? They took out the tumor yesterday but who knows when another one will grow back? I'm sorry. I shouldn't have said that. You don't even know me. But it's so strange. You look so familiar. Are you sure we haven't met?"

He searched her face. There was a TV hanging right in front of the bed. He'd obviously had a lot of time to watch the news. She saw when the recognition clicked—his eyes widened and landed on the call button for the nurse. Then his face hardened and he reached for it.

Eva let out a long breath and spoke quickly. "I didn't do it. I swear on all that is holy. My only goal—the only reason I still allow myself to walk this earth—is so I can make the killer pay. You have to believe me. I risked everything to help your son. And even if you turn me in, I want you to know that it was worth it."

Their eyes met. For a long second, she watched his internal battle.

He let go of the call button.

His body sagged into the bed and he began to cry.

She went to his side, took his hand in hers, and handed him tissues from the bedside table.

The mother in Eva emerged, and she wiped his face and stroked his hand, murmuring soothingly, "It's going to be okay. It's going to be okay. I promise."

"I want to see Dolan grow up."

When he stopped crying he swiped at his tears and then gave a strangled laugh.

"Oh my God. I'm horrified. I don't even know you. You're so kind, and you risked everything to help my family and then I lose it. I swear it's the first time I've cried since my diagnosis. I've been trying to keep it together—for Dolan and Tim—but I just couldn't any more. And then you bring me this," he gestured toward the paperwork. "How can I ever thank you?"

"Seeing your son happy is more than I could ever ask for."

A nurse walked in and spluttered, "What is going on? This is not visiting hours."

Eva pulled her baseball cap lower and ducked her head, brushing past the woman as she exited.

Back at her new home, she spent the rest of the day training and meditating, preparing herself for the battle of her life. Her wounds had only just healed. She would not be up to her normal prowess and strength, but there was no time to waste.

Tonight, well after midnight, she'd leave. Arriving before dawn was always the best way to catch the enemy unawares. She'd learned this in Sicily. Three in the morning might be the witching hour, but four in the morning was the hour of death. At least for the Queen of Spades. She made a mental note to stop and get a deck of playing cards. It'd be nice to leave her calling card so that those back in Sicily knew exactly who had killed their beloved and sacred lo scannacristiana.

Her vengeance had been postponed for far too long.

After drinking a green smoothie for dinner, Eva decided to turn in early. Back in Sicily, when her life depended on waking up at a certain time, she had programmed herself to sleep—and rise—on command. Even though it was still light out, she was sound asleep by seven, knowing she would pop up effortlessly at two.

24

"I want to come home."

At his own words, relief flooded his body. Although he had spent most of his life aching to murder a Santella, he'd realized the night before that he could have it all. He would do as The Arm wished and secure his future as a made man—a man of honor—in Sicily. He would have Eva taken out in prison. He'd already made the arrangements with the Latino gang that ruled the California prisons. They'd promised that before the light left Eva's eyes, she would know that she was dying for the death of his father, Carlo Canucci, and his bride, Malena.

"My heart aches for Sicily," he said.

The Arm grunted. "You are a true Mafioso, my son. And you shall be home soon."

"Tonight," Vincenzo said. "It is all in place. There is a red-eye flight out of LAX. I'd like to be on it." He spoke and then held his breath for a second waiting for a reply.

"It shall be done."

Vincenzo was filled with relief. "Thank you."

"Do not fail in this last, most crucial step in your mission."

The Arm hung up.

Vincenzo felt a chill race through him. If he did fail, he knew the consequences.

But failure was not an option.

He was the most accomplished assassin in all of Italy.

Vincenzo pulled on plastic gloves. He had a long night ahead of him before he boarded that flight to Sicily. The living was easy there. His expertise was saved only for the most important jobs. The rest of the time he could live the hedonistic lifestyle he had missed so much the past year.

He wanted his wife, Concetta's, warm, soft bosom to curl up against at night. He wanted the pasta fagioli that she made best and just for him. He wanted to see the sparkle in his mama's eyes when she handed him a hunk of bread to "test" the Sunday sauce.

He yearned to go back to a life where he could lie on the beach in the sun with his children. Mamma mia, he missed his children so much. Seeing their little faces on a screen was not enough. Carlo was seven now—a little man who worked hard to help his mother while his father was gone. And his oldest daughter, Malena, was turning thirteen this year. And little Rosa...his baby. The love of his life. She was now four. He'd missed so much of her life this past year, so many important milestones. It brought a tear to his eye.

"I do it all for you," he said, picking up the photograph of his family he kept near his bed and gently placing it in a duffel bag with the rest of his belongings.

He wanted his life back. Soon. He just needed to catch that plane.

Two hours later, he surveyed his work.

A bottle of chianti was set on the table with two wine glasses.

It needs one final touch, he thought. He carefully extracted two plastic baggies from his duffel bag. Each contained strands of long, dark hair. One of them contained a small clump of hair with flesh still attached to the follicles. He set this bag on the kitchen counter. He'd save that for later. He would smear it in blood and put it in her hand.

He opened the second baggie and, using tweezers, plucked out

INDIVIDUAL STRANDS OF LONG HAIR. These he placed in strategic places— one on the back of an upholstered chair, one on the bathroom sink, one on a pillow in the bedroom.

Then he picked up his duffel bag and put it in the corner by the back door along with a bag of trash. He would have to keep the gloves on. It might tip her off, but it was a chance he'd have to take. He straightened the wine glasses on the table and dimmed the lights.

At that moment, the first of the fireworks erupted, celebrating the tail end of the regatta out in the dark ocean before them. The display filled the trailer with multi-colored lights and nearly drowned out the knock at the door. He glanced at his watch. Perfect. Plastering a smile on his face, he opened the door.

"Krystal! I'm so glad you could make it. You're right on time. The Regatta celebration has just begun."

25

LOS ANGELES

From the vista point on the highway, Eva could look out over the trailer park just north of Laguna Seca.

The nearly full moon made the soft swell of waves in the distance sparkle.

A bright night was both an advantage and a hindrance. She could creep around without a flashlight, but it also heightened the risk of someone seeing her.

It was also eerily quiet. The only sounds were the lapping of the waves on the beach below and the occasional car passing behind her on Highway 1.

Driving her vehicle down the gravel road to the trailer park would be too loud. She needed stealth. She would have to walk. The thick, gripping treads on her boots would make it easy to scale the hillside that dropped down into the development. It was steep, but if she grabbed branches and bushes, she could steady herself. The thin leather gloves she wore to hide her fingerprints would protect her hands against scrapes and cuts.

Before she locked her car, she patted herself down, feeling her weapons for reassurance. She had two long swords crisscrossing in

. . .

THE HARNESS AT HER BACK. A thigh sheath held her favorite dagger. Another holster held her Glock snug up against her ribcage, and a smaller Ruger was tucked into its holster inside her boot.

Traversing the hill was somewhat unwieldy with her swords, but she knew she might need them. Vincenzo may very well have been trained in Gladiatura Moderna. But she was fairly certain she was better.

However, one gunshot would end any battle on that front. Her hope was to take him out with a blade and prevent the attention gunfire would bring.

Once she was on the level ground close to the line of trailers, she counted down from the one closest to where the road ended at a visitor parking lot. From there, a road behind the trailers led to small driveways to each one, dead-ending at the cliff. Her eyes were trained on the seventeenth trailer in from the parking lot.

Keeping behind the trailers and to the east of the long driveway, she made her way toward the trailer. As she did, she kept one eye trained on the mobile homes she passed. One had a light on, but she couldn't see inside. Another window was tinted blue from a TV screen, and she heard the mumbled laughter of a sitcom.

But as she drew closer, she verified that the seventeenth mobile home was dark.

Unlike some of the other trailers that had vehicles parked in front of them or under a carport, this trailer's small parking spot was empty.

Eva's heart thudded. This could mean everything. Or nothing.

26

He watched with binoculars as she crept around to the front of the trailer. He started the ignition on his beat-up Land Rover and pulled onto the highway as he punched the numbers on the disposable phone.

"911. What is your emergency?"

He spoke through the mask, which disguised his voice. "Eva White is at the Rocky Point Trailer Park in Laguna Beach.

Number 17."

27

Eva crept toward the closest window, but as she neared, she saw it had a thick curtain obscuring any view or interior light.

She followed the small stone path leading to the front of the trailer, which faced the ocean. The curtains here were wide open, and as Eva looked inside, she gasped and drew back in horror. The room —a combination dining room and kitchen—was filled with the soft glow of candlelight, but the flickering candles revealed a macabre scene. At first, Eva couldn't make sense of what she was looking at. Then it suddenly clicked.

The body of a woman, missing most of her face and head, was slumped in a café table chair. Behind her, bits of brain and hair and flesh were plastered on the trailer wall.

Eva yanked on the sliding glass door, though she knew it was too late.

And although she thought she knew who the woman was, she pushed that thought aside. Vincenzo could still be here waiting for her. There was no time to do anything but hunt. Her fingers looped through the opening to the sliding glass door.

. . .

AS THE DOOR SLID OPEN, she reached for her gun, letting it lead as she stepped past the body and searched the rest of the trailer. The place was empty. In the small bedroom, the bed was neatly made. The bathroom was spotless. Another candle left eerie shadows on the wall. Eva ventured back into the living room and kitchen area. As she did, she came up behind the woman's destroyed head. Lying beside the body was Krystal's ubiquitous red Kelly handbag.

Poor Yates. Even a terrible mother might be better than a murdered one.

Suddenly feeling weak and dizzy, Eva paused and clutched the hallway doorframe, trying desperately not to be sick.

Her eyes scanned the grisly scene. She tried to take it in clinically and not emotionally: 1970s furniture. Blood. Brain on the walls. A glass table with a bottle of wine and two wine glasses.

Her mind tried to put the pieces together. And as she drew closer, Eva saw that there was something that looked like a clump of seaweed in the woman's hand. Oh, my God. A hunk of black hair torn out by the roots. Eva involuntarily raised her hand to her head where the wound has barely scabbed over.

Eva frantically searched the rest of the trailer, looking for more planted evidence that would lead to her. As she did, all she could think over and over was:

All this death. And it was all her fault.

Then she heard the sirens.

28

Los Angeles

Eva ran along the beach to the north. On the drive down, she'd seen a small inlet with a few homes. It was her only chance of escape.

She'd tossed the hunk of her hair into the sea as she ran on the wet sand, but she knew Vincenzo probably left other evidence pointing to her—evidence that wasn't so obvious or as easy to find.

The vehicle was a casualty. Luckily, she didn't think it could be traced back to her or her home.

As she ran, more emergency vehicles raced by on the highway above. She came upon an outcropping of land and rocks that cut off the sand, separating the trailer community from the beach houses just north of it. Eva waded into the sea but was soon swept off her feet and yanked under and out toward the horizon. When she surfaced, she frantically tried to keep her head above water as the waves continued to pound into her and suck her under. Beneath the surface she tossed and turned but managed to kick off her boots. By the time she was thrust upward again, she was gasping for air. With only seconds to act, she reached behind her and unclasped the holster securing her long swords to her back. With relief, she felt their weight slip off her into the water.

The next wave didn't suck her down, it just crashed over her. She managed to bob on the surface, but every time she tried to swim to shore, she was sucked out to sea again.

A riptide.

She swam parallel to land until she saw lights from the housing community. This time when she headed for shore, her efforts were successful. She pulled herself onto the sand and collapsed, panting and shivering from the cold. After a few seconds, she hauled herself to her feet and stumbled toward the nearest house. If it had an alarm system she was screwed. She hoped that the residents believed the gate at the end of their drive would be enough to keep out a common burglar. But as she neared, a light flicked on inside. She ducked back behind the outcropping of rocks. She waited there for an hour, shivering. Her adrenaline had kept her going all night and now she was crashing. She tried not to fall asleep in her tiny alcove. Just a little bit longer, she told herself.

Her patience was rewarded. As soon as the faintest pink of dawn lit the sky, she heard a door slam and a car started. She watched and waited until a beige sedan pulled out of the driveway with a woman behind the wheel. She kept her eye on the vehicle and didn't rise from her hiding place until she saw it heading toward the main road.

Eva waited for the car to exit through the gated driveway, then ran toward the home, knowing perfectly well there might be somebody else still inside. She had a soggy Ruger still in her holster clunking against her thigh as she padded with bare feet. Her other weapons had all been swept out to sea. She crept up to the house, stopping every so often to listen for noises. She looked under large rocks, flowerpots, and on the door and window sills, looking for a hidden house key. Nothing.

She instead searched for something she could use to pick the lock. A small, flexible piece of metal did the trick.

The door clicked open easily. Before stepping inside, she scanned the adjacent walls for the flashing lights of an alarm. When she didn't see anything, she swung the door open, put one foot inside, and listened. Nothing. She stepped inside and gently closed the door. A few steps away was a laundry room. She saw a neat stack of folded clothes on top of the dryer. Eva stripped out of her wet clothes and rummaged through the still-warm clothes. She selected a pair of black yoga pants, a long-sleeve, purple T-shirt and a fleece pullover. On the floor was a pair of sand-caked running shoes. She found some socks and slipped them on. The shoes were two sizes too big. She tied them tight. They'd work. A large bag containing smaller plastic bags hung on a hook in the laundry room. She grabbed one and stuffed her wet clothes into it, re-stacked the laundry so it looked like it did when she'd found it, and then went to search the rest of the house. When she was sure it was empty, she poked her head into the garage, hopeful there might be another car she could hotwire. There wasn't.

She'd have to try another house.

She grabbed her bag of wet clothes and opened the back door. She took one step outside and froze. Down the road, she saw two police cars and a dark blue sedan. The sedan looked like the one she'd seen him get out of when she first saw the news report on her family's murder.

Heart pounding, she ducked back inside. She was trapped.

She crept upstairs and watched from a window as the detective and a woman in a suit knocked on the door of a house down the road. After a few minutes, they returned to their car and pulled to the next house. When they were only two houses away, Eva could see their faces clearly. The detective had dark circles under his eyes that she hadn't noticed before. The woman was pretty with small lips and huge eyes. As they walked back to the car, Detective Collins put his hand on her lower back, guiding her. Oh, so that's how it was. Eva's eyes narrowed. Interesting. There was no ring on his left finger.

The sedan pulled midway between the neighbor's house and the house she was in before getting out again.

From her vantage point, she had a clear view of the front porch of the neighbor's house. She watched as they knocked and waited. The woman stuck two cards into the doorframe and they turned toward the house she was in.

Thirty seconds later she heard pounding on the door below.

"Police." She froze.

After a few minutes, she watched as Detective Collins and his colleague walked back to their vehicle. At the last minute, with his hand on the handle of the driver's side door, Detective Collins glanced up to the second story window where she stood.

She froze. They locked eyes. Time stood still. Eva held her breath.

The detective gave the slightest, nearly imperceptible nod and turned away, opening his car door. She shrank back into the shadows of the room, hyperventilating, her heart racing. A second later, she heard both car doors slam and then the sound of the engine grew fainter as they drove away.

She dared to look through the window again. The police cars and the detective's vehicle exited the gated community and headed north on the highway above the housing development.

Twenty minutes later, Eva pulled out of the neighbor's garage in a brand-new Mercedes convertible. Before she left, she pulled into the spot where the detective's car had been parked. She stared up at the window. She could clearly see a painting of the ocean on the far wall of the room.

She shook her head. He'd seen her. And he'd let her go. What that meant she didn't know, but she didn't want to push her luck.

As she pulled onto the highway, she relished the feeling of the wind on her face. She found a large scarf on the passenger seat and tied her hair back. She'd also donned some cat-eye sunglasses she'd found attached to the visor. They would serve as a makeshift disguise.

A few miles up the road, Eva saw a sign for a small cafe and briefly considered pulling in to get some food and coffee. She was exhausted and struggled to keep her eyes open. At the last minute she realized it was a foolish idea.

And it was a good thing too.

As she zoomed by, Detective Collins and his colleague emerged from the café, clutching steaming coffees. Out of the corner of her eye, she saw Collins stop and stare at her vehicle as she drove past. She kept her gaze straight ahead, but she could feel the detective's eyes on her. She kept her eyes glued on the rearview mirror, but the detective had turned away. He didn't seem to be in a hurry to get to his car. That was twice. She wasn't going to count on his complicity a third time.

29

SICILY

There was nothing on the news about Eva Lucia Santella.

Vincenzo had spent the morning drive from the Milano
airport to Sicily searching every Los Angeles news outlet and even
checked the LAPD website and Twitter feed for any mention of the Laguna
Seca murder. Not a bloody word.

He threw his coffee cup splattering its contents all over the back of the
livery car.

He leaned over and poured himself a shot of ouzo and downed it. And
then another.

The last thing he wanted to do was turn around and get on another flight
to America. He had hoped to never see that ugly, capitalist, materialistic
country again.

He'd half expected her to follow him to Sicily on the next flight after his,
but so far three days had passed without a word. If she was as smart as he
believed, she'd be coming after him here, their childhood home that was a safe
haven for him but a dangerous battlefield for her.

He hoped she came soon. He had one last card up his sleeve for the
Queen of Spades.

30

Los Angeles

"I told my dad you probably didn't like vegetables and that he should get you donuts for dessert. I follow the LAPD on Twitter, and they really do go to Dolly's Donuts, so..." Dolan trailed off. He opened the door to his house.

Eva frowned and Dolan grimaced. "I'm sorry," he said.

She crouched down in front of him on the front porch. "No, it's not that. It's just that I've misled you about my job, and I feel awful about it."

"You're not a cop?"

Now it was her turn to blanch. "No. I am not a cop. I'm sorry I lied to you. I do some things that police officers do. But other things I don't. I do investigate people doing bad things, but I don't arrest them or put them in jail."

Dolan nodded. "So, like a private detective maybe?"

"I'm not a private detective, either. But yes, you could say my job is a little like that as far as investigating goes." "Okay." He shrugged. "Want to see my house?" And like that, the conversation was over.

Eva followed him inside. The house was modern and sleek with small windows in the front facing the city below and large windows in the back facing a swimming pool and wooded area that butted up against the hills.

The hallway opened up into a great room. Dolan's art was framed on the walls next to what looked like a De Kooning, and his toys were scattered everywhere.

She heard voices and laughter and soft jazz coming from another room.

"This is like our living room area," Dolan said.

A massive table in the great room was covered in various Lego projects. Eva grabbed for the doorframe as a wave of grief hit her. Again, she couldn't help but think that Lorenzo and Dolan would've been fast friends. But this time, the thought didn't feel like a stab to the heart. Instead, a bittersweet wave of sadness fell over her. It was the first time she was able to think of Lorenzo and want to smile instead of crawl into an open grave and never come out. It was a step.

"Eva?"

"I'm sorry," she said, swiping at a lone tear trickling down her cheek. "I was just thinking of another little boy."

Dolan looked up at her, but she quickly brushed by him, turning away from the table and saying, "I'm just so happy your dad is home from the hospital."

"Yeah. Me too." Dolan grinned. "He's in the kitchen with Tim. That's my dad's husband. Guess what? I don't have to see my mom anymore. Tim is going to adopt me. Oh shoot, I think we were going to surprise you and tell you. That's what we're celebrating—the adoption."

"That is fantastic news."

She followed Dolan into a small kitchen.

Jonathan turned with a smile. "So, glad you could make it. It's great to see you again."

Dolan gave her a sharp look.

"We met the other day," Jonathan said.

"Oh."

"But I haven't had the pleasure," Tim said. He came over and kissed Eva on both cheeks. "Ciao bella."

"Parli italiano?" she said.

"No," he said in English. "I wish. I studied it in college and spent a year in Florence. I'm an art historian."

"Aha," Eva said. "That explains this amazing art collection."

"Let me show you around. Jonathan?"

He waved them on. "Go. I'm just finishing up some final touches.
Dolan can help me, right buddy?"

"Sure, Dad."

AFTER DINNER, the three adults lingered over wine and conversation.
Dolan asked to be excused to play video games. "It's the weekend, right? So
can I?"

"Sure."

Dolan turned to Eva. "Want to come play a game with me?"

She looked at Jonathan. "I was going to help clean up."

Jonathan shook his head and waved her off, but he turned to
Dolan. "One game. We have some adult stuff to talk about."

"Okay," Dolan said, grumbling. "One game."

Inside the game room, Dolan showed her how to put on the virtual reality
glasses.

"If I puke, I'm blaming you," she said. She heard him laugh.

When she was done, she took the goggles off. "That was awesome.
Thanks for showing me."

"Sure." He grinned.

But something about this smile was slightly sad.

"How are you doing, Dolan?" Eva asked.

He looked up. "Good. I'm glad my dad's okay."

"Me too. Listen, I haven't heard back about the DNA..." She trailed off.

Dolan looked down at the carpet. "I don't care anymore."

Eva stood. "Hey, if you ever need someone to talk to, just let me know.
You have my number now."

"Okay." He was quiet.

"You sure everything is okay?"

"It's just that you seem really sad. Like when you talked about that other
boy you know," Dolan said. "It's like you're trying to be happy and cheerful,
but you seem so sad."

She crouched and met his eyes. "I'm not going to lie to you, Dolan. I am
sad. Almost all the time. Something really bad happened, and I think I'll
always be sad."

He frowned for a second and then his eyes widened. "Do you want to know what I do when I'm sad?"

"Sure."

"My dad told me this. And it works. Really it does. When I feel sad, I find someone who needs my help. Like someone who is sadder than me. Or who has maybe a rougher life than me. Sometimes if I'm really sad, my dad will take me down to volunteer at the soup kitchen. And you know what? When I'm done, I'm not sad anymore. So maybe when you are really sad, you could do something like that.

I mean, heck, I'd go with you."

Eva smiled. "You're a true friend, Dolan."

He grinned.

Eva knew she had to tell Dolan she was leaving. When she'd returned home after the trailer park incident, the first thing she'd done was to hack into Vincenzo's email account—the one under his fake name, Nikos Alexopoulos.

It still only contained a few emails from the academy. She was about to click out of the account when she remembered something she'd seen in a spy movie that she and Matthew had watched. Two people had left messages for each other in the drafts folder of their email accounts.

But when she checked the drafts folder, she didn't find anything. However, when she idly clicked on the spam folder. It contained one email—from an airline. She opened it. It showed that Vincenzo, under the name Nikos Alexopoulos, had earned an additional 1,400 airline miles with his recent purchase. Boom. It only took a phone call pretending to be his wife trying to use the airline miles to learn that Nikos had flown back to Sicily the night of Krystal's murder.

Eva immediately made plans to return to Sicily.

Tonight, she would say her goodbyes. She wasn't sure if she would ever return to Los Angeles, but she would not reveal that small detail.

"Listen, I'm going to tell your dad this in a few minutes, but I have some business in Italy and am leaving in a few days. If you need me, my cell phone will still work, but I won't be at the house, okay?"

Eva had rigged a permanent cell phone that would bounce her whereabouts around the globe numerous times so people could reach her, but nobody would ever be able to track her.

"Okay."

When Eva returned to the kitchen, Tim handed her a glass of red wine. "We've been saving this for four years."

She took a sip. "Oh, it's lovely."

"Besides celebrating the upcoming adoption and wanting to thank you for your help, I invited you here for another reason," Jonathan said. "There's something else I wanted to talk to you about."

Eva tilted her head, curious.

"Dolan doesn't know this, but I'm in a support group for parents and guardians of children who have been abused. I've made a few good friends there, and it's really helped me a lot. They teach us skills to be attentive parents and ideas on how to handle effects of the abuse that might crop up as the kids get older. It's really great. And the parents, we've all bonded. I guess nobody really understands unless they've been there, right?"

Eva nodded.

Jonathan took a deep breath. "My friend, Julie. She needs your help."

Eva felt the frown spread across her face. No way. She was leaving for Sicily in two days to track down the man who killed her family. She didn't have the time, energy, or desire to help some stranger.

"I know I have no right to come to you with this. But I didn't know where else to go. Her husband—the abuser—works in the district attorney's office. He's protected not only by the prosecutors but also by all the cops on the force. Nobody believes Julie. Or if they do, they're afraid enough of him to keep their mouths shut. The problem is, a judge is about to rule on custody arrangements. And here's the thing—the judge is crooked too. He takes graft on the side. Julie has proof of it. But she worries if she brings it up, they'll punish her. The judge knows she knows. He's going to rule against her anyway. She's desperate. She's ready to kidnap her daughter and flee the country, but her husband is suspicious and is having her followed twenty four-seven."

"Jonathan, I just told Dolan this—I'm leaving for Italy in a few days. I'm not sure when I'll be back."

His face fell. "I understand. I knew it was a lot to ask. I know," he glanced at Tim. "We know that the police are still after you." Eva shot a glance down the hall towards Dolan's room.

"Don't worry, he doesn't know," Jonathan said. "I apologize. I never should've asked you to do something that might put you in jeopardy of being caught."

"It's fine." Eva nodded somewhat curtly.

"Is there anything we can do to help?" Tim said. "To help clear your name?"

"I was set up by a pro," Eva said. "At this point, I think the detective might actually believe me. But it's going to be hard for him to

prove it. At least I have a bead on where the real killer is." "That's why you're going to Italy?"

She nodded.

"How are you getting there? I'm sure you're on every no-fly list out there. No offense," Jonathan said.

"I'm sneaking into Mexico and will take a flight out of Cabo San Lucas."

Saying the name sent a pang of pain through her. She had such wonderful memories of her honeymoon there, where she and Matthew had sunbathed, whale watched, snorkeled, and watched sunrises from a private villa far off the tourist strip.

"Sneaking in? Ironic, right? Most people do the opposite." He stood and poured her more wine. "Again, I'm sorry I asked. I just didn't know where else to turn."

As he spoke, Eva couldn't help but think about what Dolan had told her earlier. The way to cure sadness was to help someone else who was less fortunate. It was her salvation. Suddenly Eva knew she would help. She had to help. Not just to help her with her own sadness, but because she couldn't allow a child to suffer if it was within her power to do something.

"What do you want me to do?" she asked.

"I don't know," Jonathan said.

Eva stared at him for a few seconds. She picked up her wine glass and drained it before saying, "Consider it done."

31

CABO SAN LUCAS

Eva woke early the morning of her flight. She slipped out of her hotel room while it was still dark and made her way down to the sandy beach a block away.

Her hotel was in the heavily touristed area of Medano Beach, which was not far from the marina but very far away from the private villa where she and Matthew had stayed during their honeymoon. However, one of their favorite restaurants was nearby. Pausing at the entrance to the beach between two restaurants, Eva plucked her sandals off her feet and looped the straps through her fingers.

Just as her bare feet hit the cool sand, the first broad strokes of orange and petal pink glowed in the eastern sky. She made her way down to the wet sand, avoiding the soft waves lapping onto shore reflecting the golden sunrise.

As she walked along the beach, she felt the shadowy presence of the restaurant looming to her left. She kept her eyes straight ahead, refusing to look up at the large deck where she and Matthew had spent several evenings sipping margaritas. It would hurt too much to do so and would accomplish nothing.

That life was over. She was no longer that person. She was no longer

Matthew's wife or Alessandra and Lorenzo's mother. She was not even Eva Lucia Santella anymore. Not really.

She was the Queen of Spades.

And on her airline ticket, she was Lucia Michaud.

Before leaving, she'd spent her two last days in America making sure Julie's husband realized what a terrible idea it was to seek custody of his child. Waking up to cold steel pressed against your nutsack by a masked woman will do that to you.

In just a few short hours, she'd be on board her flight. And by this time tomorrow, after two quick stops, she'd land in Rome. From there, she'd rent a car and drive to Sicily.

She couldn't wait.

32

ITALY

Eva kept her huge, dark sunglasses on the entire flight.

After the plane landed on Italian soil and the passengers came to their feet, Eva hoisted her black leather backpack onto one shoulder. The woman across the aisle smiled at her, but Eva kept her face stoic.

She was not here on pleasure, and she had no idea how many people still knew about the hit on her life. To avoid the woman sitting beside her during the long flight, she had pretended to sleep. The one time the woman tried to strike up a conversation, Eva had answered in Arabic—just in case the woman spoke Italian. Even though she looked like the average Midwestern grandmother, you never knew.

Striding through the airport, Eva realized that for the first time in a dozen years, she didn't stand out. There were numerous other women with long dark hair, black sunglasses and all-black clothing.

Maybe this would be easier than she thought.

After paying cash to rent a convertible Fiat, Eva set off south toward Sicily.

By the time she got to the ferry crossing the water to her homeland, she was exhausted. Rather than force an encounter before she was ready, she decided to rent a hotel room and get a fresh start in the morning.

She'd purchased a dagger and long sword on the drive down, detouring an hour out of the way to swing by a shop she'd found online. The blades were crafted by a family that had been bladesmiths for four generations. The steel was L6, a carbon, cobalt, and nickel steel of the highest quality.

The hand-tooled leather sheaths were silky smooth like butter.

She'd tipped the old guy running the shop, kissing her fingers to compliment his artistry.

He'd blushed.

Now, safely ensconced in a hotel room overlooking the harbor and ferry boats, Eva pushed a dresser in front of her hotel room door and sank into oblivion on the lumpy bed.

The next morning when she woke, it was already close to noon, and she'd missed the morning ferry. But it was okay. She would spend the day hunting down someone who could procure her a firearm.

After eating a cornetto and downing an espresso in the hotel dining room, she ducked into the kitchen. The cook barely gave her a glance. She headed toward the busboy. Earlier, when he'd cleared her plate, she noticed a tattoo on his wrist peeking out of his long, white shirt sleeve. She caught his attention and nodded toward the back door. She slipped out into the alley and was waiting near the trash cans when he emerged. She held up a handful of euros.

"I need a gun."

He looked in both directions nervously.

"Today."

"I need one day to get it," he said.

She pulled out a few more euros.

"Today."

"I can sell you my own. That is the only way. But I will be putting my own life at risk as I walk home tonight after my shift here."

She took out another stack of euros. "Do you feel safer now?"

"Just a moment."

He walked back inside, taking her money with him.

She wasn't worried. She knew where he worked.

A few minutes later, he came back holding something wrapped in heavy, white linen napkins.

"Ammo?"

"It's loaded. You can get more over on the next street."

"Okay."

Without another glance at the boy, she turned and left. When she got to the end of the alley and was about to step into the light, she turned. He was still standing there watching. When she turned, he scrambled toward the restaurant door and disappeared.

EVA STOOD on the deck of the ferry, a large black scarf and her huge sunglasses hopefully keeping her disguised. The sight of her homeland on the horizon caused mixed emotions—excitement, sorrow, and fear.

When she stepped foot onto the Sicilian Island, Eva said a silent prayer— that the land would protect her and help her fulfill her mission of vengeance. Now that she was back in Sicily, she felt the draw of that vendetta. It was sewn into the very fabric of her being. Her DNA screamed to avenge her family's murders.

Although she longed to go to her old home, she knew it would be foolish. That would be the first place Vincenzo would wait for her if he suspected she had followed him. And she suspected that Vincenzo was reporting to some- one. The price must still be on her head.

At this point, she had to move and act as a fugitive.

Even knowing this, she also had no choice. She had to go after Vincenzo. She would start at his old family home. She would have to be stealthy and go up into the hills above and then sneak down through the forest to the back of the house. Coming into town from the road would be too obvious. Word would spread quickly about an unfamiliar woman poking around in that village.

She got back into her convertible and headed south. She would round the island the long way, stop at a small sea village for the night, and then be up before dawn. Hopefully she would be able to scout out the house before the break of day.

Close to suppertime she found a small inn that would suit her purposes. The older couple who ran the place didn't seem very tech savvy or up to date on current events. If her image had made the Italian news, they most likely would not have seen it.

They had an old-fashioned sheet for guests to sign in and told her they only took cash, didn't use credit cards, and didn't have internet.

"Perfetto!" Eva had said, telling them she was looking for a break from her high-tech job.

Eva pushed back the curtains to reveal a stunning view of the sea lit up by the moonlight. She fell into a deep sleep, programming herself to wake up in just a few hours.

33

Vincenzo was having his after-dinner espresso when the call came in on his cell phone.

"The old man at the inn outside of Marsala says she is there."

"Right now?"

"Yes."

"Get someone over there. I want her followed."

"No need. She is going to your childhood home, Vincenzo. I am certain."

"You are right."

From the minute he landed on Sicilian soil, Vincenzo had put out the word that Eva Lucia Santella might be coming home.

He'd been right.

He sat for a moment. His wife walked by and put her hand on his arm, smiling. He stubbed out his cigar and exhaled loudly. "I will handle this alone," he said into the phone.

"Are you sure?"

"Yes."

He hung up and reached for his wife, lifting her skirt. "Vincenzo, the children!"

"Children," he said without looking at them. "Go to your rooms. Now!"

But by the time they'd walked out, he'd changed his mind. He dismissed his wife, who scurried away to the kitchen where his mama was washing dishes.

HE MADE his way in the dark to the outcropping of rock behind his old house—the place where he took refuge when his father lost his temper. He'd hidden there the day the Santellas killed his father and ordered his mother to pack up and leave within twenty-four hours. She had called her family in Catania to come with trucks and help her. He stayed near the rock outcropping, refusing to go with her. He hadn't believed his father was really dead. He would return any minute and stop this nonsense.

But his mother had seen something in the big box that had arrived on their porch—something that had made her drop to her knees and wail. She'd tucked the box under her arm and went next door to call her family, telling him that his father was dead, and they were going to live with his Uncle Eduardo. It was a brutal, coldhearted way to break such shocking news to a young boy.

He'd run behind the house into the woods. His father couldn't be dead. He'd said goodbye to him just that morning.

After his mother found him and dragged him into the car, he only had one goal in life—to avenge his father's murder.

That desire for vengeance grew stronger when he turned eighteen, and his mother told him he was the man of the house. It was then that she'd told him what was in the box—his father's head—and a note for her to disappear unless she wanted Vincenzo to face the same fate.

As she told him, she handed him a neatly tied package. He undid the thick string with trembling fingers. Inside was his father's bloodstained shirt.

"They found it near a puddle of blood down by the docks, Vincenzo. They never found his body. But I know this shirt. Look," she pointed toward the hem. "I sewed that myself. It is your father's shirt. Now that you are a man, it is your duty to fulfill the vendetta."

But by that time, Vincenzo was already well on his way to vengeance. He'd spent the past three years cutting school to run errands for the local mob boss, Antonio Teverola, in Catania. The day he turned eighteen, he begged the boss for a bigger role.

"What can you do?" Teverola asked, squinting his eyes at the young man before him.

"I can kill."

The boss laughed. "You talk big."

"I can. Just tell me who. I will do it."

"Why so much hate?"

"It's not personal," he said. Teverola laughed uproariously, but then he sobered. "I might have something for you. It's very dangerous. If they catch you, they will kill you."

"Who?"

Teverola knew he wasn't asking about who might catch him. "Judge Gianluca Falcini. You will have to go into his chambers and do it there."

Vincenzo didn't blink. Usually, the name of the anti-Mafia prosecuting magistrate made people squirm. Or scowl. But he had

remained expressionless and said, "I need a gun." The mob boss nodded. "When?"

Teverola looked at the clock on the wall. "Tomorrow."

Vincenzo dressed like a messenger and was able to enter the inner chambers of the court by saying he had a message that only the judge could hear.

Once inside, the judge had looked up from his desk and frowned just as Vincenzo lifted the gun with the silencer and put a bullet right through the middle of the man's forehead. He then leaped out the three-story window onto a tree, shimmied down, and was gone before anyone was the wiser.

After, he lived with Antonio Teverola as his son. The mob boss made sure the boy received extensive training from the Mafia's most deadly hit men.

Vincenzo spent his days perfecting his assassin skills while secretly dreaming of the day he would return to the northern part of Sicily and avenge his father's murder.

But one day when he was twenty, he was pinched after killing a policeman's brother and sentenced to three years in prison. While there, he heard strange rumors—his childhood friend and now, most deadly enemy, Eva Santella, had become a made woman.

Her own brothers hated her, which he found fascinating, even if they were half-brothers. And her father was a joke—a dried-up, useless old man rotting away behind these very same prison walls.

Over the years, he'd tracked the Santellas. When he mentioned the Santella name to Teverola, the mob boss had ordered him "hands off." And when Teverola spoke, there was no room for argument. Those who had disobeyed him had been killed by Vincenzo himself in terrible ways.

Vincenzo knew he was the boss's favorite assassin, but he also knew he was not the boss's only assassin. And that loyalty must be a two-way street. Vincenzo had seen the cold stare when the boss had ordered him to kill his consigliere—Teverola's childhood friend and long-time confidant and advisor. The consigliere had betrayed the boss in a small way—by accepting money from a sworn enemy—but it was still a betrayal that could not go unanswered.

While in prison, Vincenzo continued to fulfill hits and killed on demand as ordered. But then the boss joked that he was doing such a good job as a hit man in prison, he might arrange for Vincenzo to serve a longer sentence. Having an assassin in prison was a boon to the business.

While Vincenzo laughed along, he was keeping tally of Teverola's insults and making plans. Because in prison he had met a soldier of Teverola's most powerful enemy— Ludovicus "Luigi the Arm" Mazzo.

A Sicilian Mafioso, Mazzo was interested in taking over and unifying Sicily under his rule. One by one, he planned to take out all the other mob bosses.

Luckily for Vincenzo, his first target was Teverola.

It was no coincidence that Mazzo's man shared a cell with Vincenzo. It didn't take long for an alliance to be forged. When Vincenzo was released, he wasted no time in killing his boss. And with that act, his reputation was forged in stone. He was "the People Slayer." He was the most cold-hearted assassin Italy had ever seen.

Meanwhile, Luigi the Arm's reach grew. He ruled over all of Southern Italy and part of Sicily. The only mob boss that stood in his way was Eva Lucia Santella.

She was the most powerful mob boss in that area. But then it seemed as if fortune smiled on him when the other mob bosses turned against her. She'd angered them by refusing to allow her organization to participate in the sex trade. Some of the bosses let that slide but when she had killed her own blood, her half-brother, there was not a single mob boss who would defend her.

Luigi the Arm said he would take care of her. He knew that taking out the powerful woman would secure his position as the leader of all the bosses.

He sent his underboss to take Eva out, but she'd been warned and had disappeared. When the underboss couldn't find her, he headed to the hills of Sicily where he thought the Arm was staying for the weekend in a secluded farmhouse.

But one of Eva's soldiers followed him.

When the underboss arrived, Luigi the Arm was not there. Only Mazzo's secret family: a woman he had loved since they were children and their love child, a beautiful nineteen-year-old promised to Vincenzo in marriage.

Once inside the wooden farmhouse, the underboss realized his mistake. He saw Eva's soldiers sneaking up and surrounding the house. Then the underboss made his last, fatal mistake by grabbing a stash of weapons and firing from each window as if an army waited inside.

Eva's men, armed with assault rifles, wasted no time destroying the structure, splintering the wood into slivers and slaughtering the underboss and the two women inside.

When Luigi the Arm found out, he couldn't even mourn publicly. Most people believed the woman and teenager had been the underboss's secret family. Only the Arm and Vincenzo could mourn their losses together. The two men made a blood oath to make Eva Santella pay if it was the last thing they did.

But when they went to seek vengeance, she'd disappeared. The rumor was that she'd fled to America.

It had taken Vincenzo and his boss years to finally find her. It was dumb luck. A young cousin of the Braccio family was on a beach in Southern California and spotted the fugitive Eva. The woman had come up from the water and entered a house on the beach.

The girl had heard the tales of the Queen of Spades after growing up in the same town. She'd even spotted her once in a local bakery. The girl had been about to go up and say hello but then became embarrassed and convinced herself she was imagining things. But she did snap a photo and showed her mother that night at the hotel. After a terse conversation between her parents, her father interrogated her about where she'd seen the woman.

The next day, Vincenzo was on a plane to Los Angeles with a new name and a plan.

His bloodthirst for Eva's head was doubly powerful—the Santella family had killed his father and the woman he'd planned to marry.

Now, back in his home country, Vincenzo couldn't believe that Eva had fallen for his trap. He would be waiting. At the rock. The place where he had once stolen a kiss from her while their parents were inside drinking grappa until the wee hours. It was his first kiss, and nothing had ever compared.

He would kiss her again today again. But it would be the kiss of death—and the sweetest kiss of his life.

34

Eva was glad for the waxing gibbous moon. It helped her see as she made her way down the steep, briar-covered hillside toward the old Canucci house. The thick tread on her boots helped her grip the dirt, but some broke free and tumbled down ahead of her. Something rustled in the bushes nearby. She froze, but it was only a small creature, not a person.

Armed with her long swords, dagger, and a gun, she was as prepared as she was going to get.

There was always the chance that a trap had been set and Vincenzo lay in wait for her at the house.

As she grew closer and could see the windows of the house, she realized that this was more likely than not. Inside one window she could see a faint glow as if from a candle. Someone was there.

She paused at the big rock where Vincenzo had kissed her so many years ago and wondered once again what had happened to turn such a sweet boy into a monster.

A twig cracked and she whirled. At the same time came a deafening noise, and a crushing weight pushed her entire body down into the ground, pressing her open mouth into the soil. The last thing she thought was that she was going to suffocate on dirt, and that was a cowardly way to die.

35

Sicily

"You have pleased me."

Vincenzo did not dare smile. He simply bowed his head slightly.

"Do you want her before..." The Arm looked down at Eva's limp body sprawled on the marble floor. Her head was thrown back. Her pulse could be seen throbbing in her neck.

Vincenzo tried to look confused, but his blood raced. He felt a fissure of excitement. Was Mazzo offering what he thought? No. It had to be a test.

"Sir?"

His boss gave him a tight smile and nodded. Another man leaned down, lifted Eva up, and threw her across his shoulder. She gave a slight moan.

Vincenzo wanted to ask where she was being taken, but it was not his concern. Not anymore. He'd brought her home and literally laid her at the boss's feet. He had returned a hero.

"I am impressed," the Arm said.

"Thank you." Again, he dipped his head slightly in a nod.

"You may go."

He looked up in surprise. He'd expected something more. Praise showered on him? A celebration? Something. He wasn't sure. The two of them had shared this vendetta—this hatred—for more than ten years, and this was it? Just a dismissal? Mazzo examined him coldly.

Vincenzo hid his fury and turned to leave.

36

Sicily

Francesca watched from the balcony above the inner courtyard. Just what was her darling husband up to? Her eyes narrowed. He'd never told her where his extreme hatred for Eva Santella came from.

Now was the time to find out. He had a meeting that afternoon in town. She would sneak into his office and read the journal she'd seen him writing in this morning. When she walked into his study, he'd been writing furiously with an evil grin on his face that she'd never seen before. When he saw her, he quickly tucked the journal into a desk drawer and locked it. Luckily, Francesca knew where he kept the key.

37

Sicily

Vincenzo whistled as he strode down the main drag in
Palermo. The salty breeze felt cool on his hot forehead, and he inhaled
deeply and smiled to himself.

It was going to be the greatest night of his life.

Finally, the Arm had called him and ordered him to attend a private gathering of the mob bosses. He said to dress sharp. Vincenzo hung up the phone
smiling. He'd waited a long time for this. Although he'd been pleased when
he was named lo scannacristiana, he'd grown weary of the life of an assassin.

He wanted to be a fat cat like Mazzo. He wanted to live in a villa overlooking the sea. He would give his wife her own master suite. He would build
an entire wing for his mama and a small home near the garden for Henrietta.
His wife would be so pleased with the villa and the riches and the jewels, she
would let him do as he pleased. Everything he'd dreamed of was going to be
his for the taking.

He'd fulfilled the greatest mission of his life, and now he would reap the
promised rewards. What luck that the dumb broad had followed him to
Sicily. It could not have been better planned. Now she was rotting deep
within the bowels of Mazzo's villa.

Eva would soon be dead. And he would soon be one of the most powerful men in all of Italy.

No longer would he have to run errands for his mama, who had sent him into town today to buy a wedge of Romano for her pasta dish. From now on, he would order his house staff to take care of such measly tasks. When his mother had first asked him to go into Palermo for her, his initial response had been anger, but then he realized he could kill two birds with one stone. He would pick up what his mother needed and have a little bit of what he needed. And right now, he needed Henrietta and what only she would offer. He needed to satisfy his lust if he were ever going to be calm at tonight's party.

Henrietta did not disappoint. He'd just left Henrietta's flat above the bar and walked quickly down the cobblestone streets and was heading toward his car when an old crone stepped in front of him on the narrow sidewalk and held up her palm to halt him. Bright eyes peeked out of a black shawl.

"Move, old woman," he'd said.

She lifted a gnarled finger and pointed it at his chest. It trembled.

He was about to bat her hand away when she spoke.

"You will never see the likes of heaven."

He froze at the words, but quickly regained his composure. He was about to shove her out of his way when two large men came and stood on either side of the woman. What the hell? He quickly dipped inside a store to his right, heart pounding. When he looked back outside, all three people were gone.

What the hell was going on? He emerged back onto the sidewalk and looked both ways but couldn't see anyone who even resembled the hunched older woman and the two burly men.

He shook his head. Maybe he'd had too much wine with Henrietta.

Even though he told himself the woman was a crazy old witch, the specter of her words draped over his shoulders like a heavy cloak as he made his way back to his wife and mother.

38

Francesca sat before her mirror, applying heavy makeup to the bruises her husband had left on her neck. The heart wrenching strains of il cuore è uno zingaro filtered out through hidden speakers in the corner of the room.

She had picked this album for a reason. It had been playing the night of their wedding, when they danced on the terrace overlooking the sea.

One lone tear slid down her cheek as she stared at herself in the mirror. That eye was also thickly caked with makeup to hide the fading, yellowish black eye beneath.

The song had also been playing the first time he hit her.

She loved him. But he would die.

His anger had gotten worse. While he used to just scream in her face, the past few months, he had taken to beating her. It had started with a slight shove onto the bed during an argument.

She'd watched as his eyes widened with the thrill of it. A week later, he struck her, sending her reeling to the ground. He would pay for lifting a hand against her. He would pay. With his life.

After reading his journal, she had seen what a truly awful man he was.

He'd lived a double life. He had kept a secret family in the hills— a simple farm girl he'd known since childhood and a secret love child. It was unforgivable. And he'd kept their murders a secret from her as well. He'd lied to her their entire relationship. And he'd spent years of his life and untold thousands to seek revenge on Eva Santella.

Francesca shook while reading the journal entries. She hated him. She hated him not only for sleeping with another woman, but for keeping a secret family. And she hated that she'd wasted so much of her life with him, turning a blind eye to his dark side. She'd put up with everything—even the occasional beating—but this was too much. He would die for this. This involved her honor. He had sullied her. Publicly? How many others had known about this over the years?

After her bruises were covered, she donned a silky golden dress. The big party was tonight. She was expected to look and act amazing, entertaining their guests. But as soon as the guests were gone, she would put her plan into action.

She leaned over and hit repeat on the operatic song. She closed her eyes and sang the words that would give her the strength to get through this night. She sang about suffering and the wound deep in her heart. How she said it was nothing, but still cried. And the line that said it all, "Per te si è fatto tard" —For you, it's too late.

39

SICILY

Eva first noticed the cold wall against her back. She was slumped, somehow sitting upright, her head hanging to her chin.

Her mind was still slightly fuzzy but clearing.

She needed to assess her situation and surroundings and do a body check.

Without opening her eyes or moving, she scanned her body, starting at the top of her head and moving downward. Her head throbbed. Her wrists ached; she didn't move them but felt something digging into them. The back of her left thigh, flung out before her, stung.

When she got to her toes, she made her way back up, this time analyzing her mood—sleepy but fraught with anxiety—and then listened intently. She heard distant rumblings above. She identified the noises: doors closing, voices, furniture scraping across floors, a vacuum. And closer, the sound of water rushing through pipes.

The air was chilly and the ground under her and the wall behind her seemed damp.

She was in a basement. But she couldn't tell if she was alone.

There might be someone else there with her. She listened for any sign of life around her, for the slightest whisper of air from someone else's breathing.

Though she heard nothing, she still waited. Finally, she opened her eyes to slits, keeping the rest of her body immobile. Her eyes scanned the room. A small bulb near the ceiling filled the room with a dim light, allowing her to make out its features.

She was in a wine cellar. The opposite wall was cave-like with a curved ceiling above a recess filled with shelves of wine. Using her peripheral vision, she saw boxes stacked to the right. Vaguely, she noted that they were labeled with various holidays: Christmas, Easter, the Feast of the Archangel Michael.

To the left, she saw a row of large, wooden cabinets.

She lifted her head. She felt cold steel on her neck. She instinctively tried to reach up to figure out what it was, but her wrists were clasped in thick steel bands. They cut into her flesh. She yanked on them. A thick chain on each one was bolted to the wall behind her. She jerked her head and was yanked back as she heard the chains on her padlocked collar jingle. The thick, steel collar was also chained to the wall behind her.

Her legs were free. She drew her knees up to her chest. Whatever had happened to the back of her thigh left a dark smear of blood in the dirt beneath where her leg had been. She managed to draw her leg up enough to gingerly prod the back of her leg with her left hand. She winced as she pressed on the wound. She felt crusty, dried blood on her torn pants. Thank God. At least the blood seemed to have clotted. That was good.

Scrunching her face, she tried to remember what had happened. How had she ended up in a basement? As the fog in her brain cleared, it came back to her quickly. She'd been creeping up to Vincenzo's old house. The last thing she remembered was being near the big rock where he had kissed her as a boy.

He must have been lying in wait or had someone else there waiting for her.

Whoever had hit her must have knocked her out. That would explain the pounding in her head and why she felt nauseous every time she moved.

She kept her knees up to her chest to stay warm. The length of the chain securing her wrists to the wall allowed her to keep her hands at her hips, but no further. She thought furiously. There had to be a way to escape.

At the same time, dread filled her. There was a hit on her life here in Sicily. Vincenzo stood to gain fame and fortune for killing her. What she didn't understand was why she was still alive. Again, he'd the chance to kill her, but hadn't.

Unless he was bringing her to someone else who would do the honors, so to speak. She didn't mind dying, but she didn't want it to be like this. Not as a helpless victim.

The sound of a throat clearing made her jump back, slamming her head against the wall behind her and sending her blood racing through her body.

"You do not seem afraid."

She whirled, as much as her neck brace would allow. The voice emerged from a shadowy corner by the row of cabinets hidden in darkness.

The man stepped into the light with a shuffling sound.

He was tall for a Sicilian, at least six feet, with his head nearing the cellar ceiling. He wore a white shirt made of some shiny fabric like silk that shimmered slightly in the light. His black trousers had a perfect crease, and his polished shoes gleamed in the dim light.

His black hair was slicked back. He raised a hand and several jeweled rings glinted as he rubbed his jaw. "You have grown into quite the beauty."

"Who are you?" Her tone was flat, disinterested. She kept her eyes hooded, watching him through her long lashes.

"You were sexy as a nubile teen, but now as a grown woman, your sexiness is unrivaled. It must be motherhood."

The words were like a knife to Eva's heart. She wanted to spit in the man's face, but he towered above her, moving closer until she was staring at his pants leg. A little closer and she could kick out his kneecaps.

"I have dreamed of this day for years, Eva Lucia Santella," he said.

"You took everything that mattered away from me."

"I have no idea what you are talking about."

Her mind raced. Obviously, he was one of her enemies from long ago. But which one. And why had he spared her life only to imprison her?

"You might be wondering why you are still alive when there is a price on your head," the man said and crouched down before her. Eva gauged the distance; he was beyond the reach of her good leg.

If he scooted any closer, she would rotate her leg and thrust her boot into his nose sending fragments of bone into his brain.

The man sighed. "I see you are not ready to talk." He started to stand.

Eva needed to keep him at her level and bring him closer. She opened her mouth and whispered. "Who are you?"

The man smiled and cocked his head. "What's that my dear? I can't hear you?"

She mumbled it again, this time lower. He leaned in. There. He was close enough.

Concentrating all her power on the heel of her foot, Eva thrust her leg up and out, aiming for the man's nose. But he drew back in time. The blow was not an instant kill as she'd intended. Instead, blood gushed from his nose. Before Eva could draw her foot back for another strike, he grabbed it and twisted, making her scream in agony. The sound was stifled by a rain of fists on her face. She gasped for air, jerking her head left and right trying to avoid the blows. But they had already moved to her chest and abdomen. She gasped for air.

She kicked at him, but the man sat on her legs, pinning her down as he pummeled her, sometimes with his fists, sometimes with an open palm. She felt the wound on her leg burst open and then a new rush of pain.

Meanwhile, he continued to strike, muttering a slew of curse words with each blow. Finally, he sat back, breathing heavily and clutching at his chest.

For a second, a glimmer of hope filled Eva. But then he smiled and stood, hands on his knees. He met her eyes.

"I'm a little out of shape. But I'll be back for more."

He frowned as he glanced down at his shirt, now spattered with blood. He ripped it off, and the buttons clattered on the floor. He wore a white undershirt. His chest heaved from his attack on her.

"I liked this shirt," he said. "It was custom made. The seamstress is the finest in all of Southern Europe." He flung the shirt to the ground near Eva. She heard the slightest sound of metal striking the floor. Eva's chest filled with hope, and she lifted her eyes to see if he had noticed, but he was still spouting off details about the shirt.

"I am having a party tonight. You are invited. But I think it's best if we bring the party to you. One man at a time. Or maybe I'll bring some chairs down so there is an audience. I will ask the men what they desire. You see, each of them has something to say to you."

He cocked his head. "The party will consist of all the mob bosses from the past. You are the pre-party before the cupola meeting tomorrow. You might have forgotten the old ways in your new life in America, but we Sicilians, we never forget a wrong. We take vengeance on those who have done us wrong. Our ancestors will haunt us if we don't. You are going to bring peace to these men who have waited much too long to fulfill this vendetta. I, for one, have dreamed of this day for years. That is why I am savoring this moment. This day."

The cupola was a group comprised of the Mafia's general staff. It was the most senior organization in the Mafia, and its members dictated who should be murdered and what crimes Mafioso would commit. It was the cupola who'd convened and ordered Eva's death so many years ago.

This man was obviously a capo mandamento—a member of the cupola and chief of the cosche—the other Mafia families in the area.

Eva shifted, trying not to look at the pool of blood seeping out from under her left leg. She needed him to leave so she could try to stop the bleeding.

He grabbed his crotch. "The anticipation is nearly as sweet as the act itself sometimes. Sometimes even sweeter. Don't you find that true?"

"Go to hell!"

She spit the words out, tasting blood as she did. She closed her eyes, waiting for the blow that was sure to come. Instead, she heard a door open and close and then footsteps and the creak of stairs.

Eva closed her eyes and nearly wept with relief but then scolded herself: If you feel sorry for yourself, you will die. If you do not stop the bleeding from your leg, you will die. If you are not strong and brave and impervious to the pain you feel right now, you will die. If you do not outsmart him right now, you will die.

Her eyes snapped open.

First things first. Distance herself from the pain and staunch the bleeding.

For a few seconds, she sat and scanned her body, lingering on the parts screaming with pain until she was able to look down on herself from afar, impassively acknowledging the pain but staying separate from it, immune to it. Her yoga and meditation practice over the past decade had paid off.

In the Bhagavad Gita, the 2,500-year-old Sanskrit text on yoga, Krishna talked about titikṣā—the art of feeling and enduring pain and suffering while remaining detached enough to not react. Eva had been working on this for five years. Now was the true test.

Leaning over, she reached for the man's discarded shirt. It was blood-stained but cleaner and more sanitary than her own clothes. Her fingertips didn't reach the shirt. She stuck her good leg out, arching her foot until her toe touched the shirt. Almost. She stretched further. Finally, she was able to scoot the shirt close enough to grasp with her right hand.

As she did, she felt something hard on the ground. Cufflinks. She used her mouth to rip them free. She dipped her head, dropped them from her mouth into her hand, and examined them.

Perfect. Something that could, at the very least, take an eye out.

She tucked them behind her, between her back and the wall.

She rolled the shirt into a strip and bent her left knee. She winced at the pain and forced herself to rise above her body again, looking down from outside the pain. Using her mouth and one hand, she managed to tie the shirt around her thigh and yanked it tight. And then tighter still.

The blood soaked right through. She was going to bleed out. She was already feeling dizzy and faint. If it was from blood loss, it was a sign that her body was going into shock and shutting down. If it was, instead, from the injuries she had just sustained, she had a chance.

Her eyes grew heavy. She fought to keep them open. An icy cold settled on her in the dank basement, making her entire body shake spasmodically. Her heart raced and she felt nauseous and overwhelmingly thirsty.

If she were to die today, let her die before this psychotic Mafioso and his cronies had their way with her. Let her die with honor. Let her deprive him of the satisfaction. With this thought, she smiled and drifted off into a shadowy haze.

40

SICILY

"Lift her. Gently. Take her other arm."

The voice was feminine and concerned. Opening her eyes, Eva saw a flash of strawberry blonde hair glinting in the candlelight.

She felt several arms on her. There was a click, and her head dropped forward. A damp washcloth was pressed to her lips. She sucked at it greedily, extracting water from it.

"Easy now."

She felt something tighten on her upper thigh. She winced in pain.

"Sorry, love. It's a tourniquet. You're bleeding something fierce." It started to come back to Eva. She was a prisoner in a basement.

She began to struggle. "Hold still. We are getting you to safety, but we have to hurry. Luigi is in the bath. We only have a short time."

Eva did a slow blink. Luigi. Ludovicus "Luigi the Arm" Mazzo.

A vague memory came back to her. Her men had tried to kill him years ago and instead killed The Arm's underboss and a woman and child at a secluded farmhouse. She blinked again, trying to take in the scene before her.

A group of women, maybe five or six of them, surrounded her.

They tended to her leg, lifted her onto a sheet, and then carried her up the stairs. She weakly gripped the side of the sheet, hoping it would not flip and send them all plummeting down the stairs. The women's faces were red with exertion.

A burst of sunlight blinded her as they reached he top of the stairs and entered a room.

"Put her in the main floor guest room. Leticia, you stay with her. Lock the door. Doctor Agnelli is on the way. Don't let anyone in but him."

"Why? Why are you doing this? He will kill you," Eva said.

"No. I am going to kill him. Tonight. In front of everyone." Eva examined the woman's face. She was dead serious.

"What is your name?"

"I'm Francesca Scalia Domenico Ribaldi." "You are Mazzo's wife?" She nodded.

"Why must you kill him?"

"He had a secret family. Your men killed them many years ago. But I only now learned of this."

That explained why Mazzo wanted her dead and why this woman was going to kill her husband. Sicilian women would tolerate just about anything except adultery. Vincenzo was another story. She still hadn't figured out the motive behind his oath of vendetta against her.

"Who is attending the party?" Eva asked.

"Nearly a dozen capo mandamentos from Sicily," she said and listed ten names. Eva recognized seven of them. "Tomorrow is the cupola. Tonight's party is to celebrate your capture."

"Is the capo dei capi going to attend?" The capo dei capi, was the godfather of all godfathers. Eva wasn't even sure who that was now.

"No. Rocco Ferraro is going to join them online." "Wow. Things have changed." Francesca smiled.

"And you must kill him tonight?" Eva asked.

"As soon as he sees you are free, he will know it is me. He will kill me for releasing you."

"Well, that's a problem." Eva's eyes narrowed. "Do you have to kill him after the party? Why not now? Before they arrive. He's in the shower, right? Can we sneak up on him?"

Francesca pointedly looked at her lying in the bed, a mixture of humor and doubt on her face.

"Okay. I see the problem," Eva said.

"The problem is that I am not a killer like you. I have never killed. Not once. I have one chance. I have a gun. I will walk up and shoot him in the back of the neck, at the brain stem where the bullet cannot miss its mark."

"I see you've done some thinking about this," Eva said.

Francesca dipped her head in graceful acknowledgment.

Eva watched her. She wore makeup that just barely disguised the many bruises in various stages on her face and neck, from blackish purple to yellow. Francesca needed to avenge herself. But there was also no reason for her to ruin her life doing so.

"I have a plan," Eva said. "You helped me. Now it's time for me to help you."

"Look at you," Francesca said. "You can barely move on your own."

"Will you agree to help me if I guarantee you that Mazzo will die, and you and I will be able to walk away and start a new life?" Francesca raised an eyebrow.

"I'm going to need some heavy firepower," Eva said. "At least one assault rifle. I'm going to give you a list of drugs. I'll need your doctor to bring them to me when he comes. And I'll need a shot of vodka."

A fiery spark appeared in Francesca's eyes, and she pulled back her shoulders.

"It will be done."

She turned to the other women. "Call the doctor, give him the list of whatever Ms. Santella says he needs to bring. Now!"

41

SICILY

Francesca leaned against the velvet wallpaper on the ballroom's east wall and surveyed the crowd. Ten of the most influential men in Italy. Ten mob bosses convened at her house for a night of debauchery before an important meeting with at least ten others in Palermo the next morning.

Soft music piped through hidden speakers. Two massive bouquets as large as Francesca adorned tables on either end of the room. A massive oak table was piled high with the best selection of food in all of Southern Europe —the finest fresh seafood crudo, comprised of briny sea urchin, red shrimp, baby squid, and salty anchovies; croquettes made with cheese and mint; a pesto pasta with sundried tomatoes and pine nuts; ricotta with honey and pistachio; gelato and cannoli and more.

Another entire table had been transformed into a bar, laden with aged wines and spirits and prosecco. There was no bartender and few staff. These men trusted no one. Too many of their enemies would love to stumble on these men all in one house. Even the polizia— maybe especially the polizia— would look at it as a great opportunity to test out a confiscated pipe bomb. The only people allowed to work the party were Luigi's manservant and two of Francesca's most trusted handmaids—Leticia and Anna.

At least that's what Luigi thought. Francesca had other plans.

Two of her most trusted men from the stables were waiting in the massive guest bedroom off the main first floor hallway for her signal.

Francesca played the part of a wallflower. The men were so busy boasting and bragging about their conquests and riches, they didn't seem to need female attention. For once.

Her husband had arranged the meeting with these southern Italian bosses to assert his dominance and to give them a piece of Eva.

Each of these men had a personal vendetta with Eva. She had taken someone from all of them. Each had been waiting years to take their vengeance.

Luigi had not told them the details; he had just told them a special gift awaited them at his house.

Earlier, he'd told Francesca to keep herself busy between eight and nine, preferably somewhere out of earshot, because she might not like what she heard.

As the clock struck eight, she waited and watched, her nerves on fire. Finally, at nearly one minute after eight, Luigi's manservant nudged him. Luigi nodded and jutted his chin toward the door. The manservant, a young man that her husband was grooming to be the next Vincenzo, was unearthly in his beauty. Francesca wondered if her husband had chosen him just for this reason. Although her husband had never expressed a predilection for men, now that she had learned he was an adulterer she wouldn't be surprised.

As the manservant slipped past, Francesca smiled at him. He wouldn't meet her eyes. Aha. He was screwing her husband. That was too bad. She'd originally considered sparing him.

As soon as he passed, she gave the slightest nod and then looked away. Leticia and Anna slipped out of the room, carrying dishes as if they were going to the kitchen.

Francesca counted to herself, regulated her breathing, and then walked over to the bar. She poured herself another glass of wine and returned to her spot near the door, pretending to sip on it. From her vantage point she could see down the main hall.

With hooded eyes, she watched her husband's manservant emerge from the door to the basement. The poor man's face was pale, and he paused, taking a deep breath and running a hand through his hair nervously before rushing back down the hall and into the ballroom. Francesca remained by the entrance, eyes lowered but trained on Luigi. He was speaking with Vincenzo, laughing heartily and slapping the dark-haired man on the back. Even from across the room, Francesca could see Vincenzo's eyes narrow at the slap.

But as soon as the manservant delivered his message, her husband whirled, scanning the room until his eyes landed on her.

"Francesca!" At his shout, everyone else in the room grew quiet.

Luigi stomped over to her, continuing to yell. "Francesca! Where is she? If you had anything to do with this, you will pay! I promise. Tell me this instant! Where is she?" His face was red. The vein in his jaw throbbed. It looked like his head was going to explode.

She hadn't expected this—a public scene. She'd thought he would take her aside in private. That was fine. She could pivot.

She plastered a huge smile on her face and turned toward the men in the room.

"Surprise!" she said. Everyone stared. "Ludovicus and I have a wonderful surprise for all of you. And I've surprised my dear husband even more by adding my own special touches. Sometimes a woman's touch is needed in matters like these, you see." Leaning toward her husband, Francesca said in a lower voice, "You are going to be so thrilled when you see what I have done for you."

"What?" He looked around. The other men raised eyebrows and snickered.

Francesca turned toward the men in the room.

"I know this is a very special night for all of you. Some of you have waited a decade to make...let's just say, to make things right. But I was thinking about it. You are all sophisticated men of superior taste."

She paused and met each man's eyes one by one. At her words, their chests puffed out, and their shoulders drew back at the flattering words.

"As I thought about tonight's festivities, I realized that you all deserve a superior experience. Much like the difference between street food and fine dining. Here at our lovely home, we insist on offering you the fine dining option.

"You don't want to tromp down to the dark and dingy basement to seek your vengeance, do you?"

"The basement?" One man sniggered.

"Yes," Francesca said. "That's where we were keeping her." At the word "her" eyebrows raised all around the room.

Again, Francesca gave a dramatic pause. The men looked at one another. "Because that was initially the plan," she said. "That's why my dear husband seems a bit surprised. I took matters into my own hands to create a five-star experience for you distinguished gentleman. Follow me."

She pirouetted and with a swish of her skirt headed toward the guest bedroom. She held her breath, waiting. Finally, her husband laughed. "God, I love that woman. She always keeps it fresh. Come on, gentlemen. I'm sure you won't be disappointed. Francesca knows how to please her man. And if she can please me, I know you will be pleased with what she has in store for you."

There were snickers and then, with relief, Francesca heard chairs scrape back as they rose to follow.

While the others lined up behind her and her husband, Francesca flung open the door to the room. At first only she and her husband stood in the doorway, taking in the scene.

Soft, sexy Latin music filtered out. Eva sat propped against a mass of pillows on the bed. She wore a blood red ball gown that was spread out in massive puffs around her. Her black eyes were lined with kohl. Her breasts nearly spilled out of the gown's deep-cut neckline. Ten velvet chairs were lined up at the foot of the bed. Mirrors had been propped up against the other three walls. Red rose petals were scattered on the floor. Every available surface was covered with flickering white candles.

Luigi roared with pleasure. "This! This is marvelous." He leaned over and kissed Francesca on the mouth, leaving a sloppy wetness all the way down to her chin.

But then he drew back, and his eyes narrowed. He reached for a gun inside his jacket. "She is not bound." His voice was wary.

Francesca quickly reached for his forearm. "It's okay. We've come to an agreement. She will not struggle. She knows that she is going to die tonight. I have convinced her to cooperate so it will be easier for her."

Eva hung her head slightly and nodded, exuding an air of defeat.

Reaching up to whisper in her husband's ear, Francesca added, "And just to be sure, I have drugged her as well. She will comply. She will concede to your every wish. This is better, my love. This way the men will see your restraint and your control over even the mighty Queen of Spades as she bows to your will and word. It will glorify you in front of them. It will seal your status and power."

He pushed his wife away, but his shoulders drew back and a faint smile crept onto his lips.

"Men. Please come in. Allow me to introduce the Queen of Spades."

The men rushed into the room. Some shouted and laughed, others spewed foul names at the woman in the bed.

Francesca spread her arms. "Please come in and have a seat. I know you are all sophisticated men," she said. "I thought you were deserving of this. Rather than everyone huddled in a basement taking turns—because that's the other part of the surprise—you each get a turn with her. And I hope you're not shy, because we're all going to watch. It will be the final humiliation for this whore." Francesca leaned over and spit.

Her husband laughed. "Enough of that." Then Francesca turned toward Vincenzo.

"Vincenzo, we owe this moment to you. Thank you." He blushed but couldn't draw his eyes away from Eva.

"Be a dear and go grab Luigi's cognac from the study," Francesca said.

Vincenzo balked, but Luigi gave him a look. He disappeared down the hall.

Luigi noticed that two handmaids were in the room. While the men sat in chairs facing the foot of the bed, each woman was pressed up against a wall flanking the sides of the bed. They both wore elegant dresses and stood with their hands behind their backs.

Luigi frowned and said in a low voice, "Must they remain in the room?"

"Yes, my dear. They have a very important job here tonight." He gave her a quizzical look.

"To take care of those waiting in line."

He roared with laughter. He grabbed her face and kissed her long and hard. "You are a gem. Nobody could have such a fine wife as you."

One of the men grunted, and her husband looked over and gave him an exaggerated wink.

"Why don't you sit here, my love," Francesca said, gesturing to the largest chair at the end of the bed, nearest the door. "We will go in order starting at the other end."

She leaned down to his ear. "I know how you like to watch. By the time it is your turn, you will be on fire."

Her husband stuck his hand in the scoop neck of her dress and groped her before she could draw away. He moaned. "This is the greatest day of my life. Thank you."

"It will most definitely be a memorable one," she said and moved toward the door. "Shall we begin?"

"What about Vincenzo?" her husband asked.

"That man child? Do you think he deserves her again? He took her already in L.A."

Luigi's face grew red with fury. "What?"

Francesca nodded. "Sorry. He never told you this?"

"Lock the door."

Francesca turned to the door with a small smile her husband could not see. As she walked to the door, she met Leticia's eyes. The other woman stood expressionless against the wall. Near the door was a small table with an ice bucket on it. A bottle of champagne peeked from the top. Francesca closed and dead bolted the door and reached deep into the ice bucket.

At the noise, her husband's head swerved sharply her way. But she had already drawn out the Glock. She took two strides toward him and fired at point blank range, striking her husband between the eyes. At the same moment, Eva withdrew one of two assault rifles tucked under her billowing gown and began to fire. As the room erupted in a cacophony of gunfire, Francesca kept her eyes trained on her husband. His mouth hung open as he fell to the floor, dead. Everything happened in slow motion. Distantly, Francesca was aware of gunfire and bodies jerking and twitching and blood and brains and flesh flying everywhere.

It seemed an eternity but must have only been a few seconds before normal sound and movement resumed for Francesca. She whipped her head around to make sure her handmaids were okay.

Leticia and Anna stood frozen, their guns at their sides.

Nine men, including her husband, were slumped either on the floor or in their chairs. But one man in the middle cowered, clutching his chest. Sweat dripped down his brow. His glossy eyes were locked on the woman in the red dress.

Francesca turned toward the bed. Eva was on her knees, leaning forward, with the assault rifle pointed at the man.

"Please." The word came out garbled.

"I spared you for only one reason," Eva said. "Go to the Council tomorrow morning and tell them what happened here." The man nodded fervently.

Eva lowered her gun. "And when you do, give them this message:

The Queen of Spades sends her regards."

The man nodded again but stayed seated, staring.

"Leave now before I change my mind." Eva's voice was low and deadly as she gestured toward the door with the assault rifle. The man scrambled to his feet, tripped over the dead man's slumped body beside him, and nearly fell as he scrambled to the door. His hands shook wildly as he unlocked the dead-bolt. Then he was gone through the open doorway. He could be heard retching as he ran away.

Eva briefly met Francesca's eyes before collapsing face first onto the bed.

Francesca ran over to the bed and flipped Eva overlooking for a gunshot wound.

"I'm not shot," Eva said, opening her eyes. "But I need something. That hypodermic needle the doctor left...it has adrenaline in it. Stick it in my neck. Now."

Francesca hesitated and Eva repeated firmly, "Now!"

As soon as the syringe was pressed, Eva sat up. She smoothed her skirt down before swinging her legs over the side of the bed. She smiled, but there was murder in her eyes. "Take me to him. Now."

42

Eva unlocked the door, slipped inside, and closed it behind her.

She locked the door behind her. Vincenzo stood with his back to her, his shoulders slumped, his head down.

Candlelight filled the room, just as she had ordered. The wax globes sat on the floor, lining the walls of the room. No candlestick holders. Everything that might be used as a weapon—table lamps, furniture, even a hanging light fixture, had been removed from the room.

She was surprised he hadn't extinguished the candles, to try to create an advantage of darkness when she came for him.

"Do you like to play cards?"

Eva was tired of playing around. She was going to take no chances in killing this man tonight. It was long overdue. But she wanted him conscious when she did so. She wanted him to know that his life was hers for the taking.

Before he could react, she was behind him with the blade against his throat.

He inhaled sharply.

Sixty seconds later, Vincenzo Canucci lay dead at her feet.

She placed a Queen of Hearts playing card face up on his chest and then turned on her heel and left without a backward glance.

As soon as she returned to the hall, Eva collapsed into Francesca's waiting arms.

"Get the car now!" Francesca screamed.

43

Sicily

"She's fine. Her only wounds are cuts and bruises and the large laceration on the back of her thigh. I stitched it up," the doctor said.

Francesca sighed with relief. Despite the doctor's reassurance, the blood all over his floor seemed evidence of another crime scene.

"I'm sorry about the mess," Francesca said.

"It's not the first time."

"Will they be able to tell you helped me?"

The doctor shook his head. "Unless someone in your party says something, I am safe."

Francesca exhaled. "I promise that will not happen. I will order their silence. Disobedience will mean death."

"Wow. I didn't know you cared." He winked as he said it.

"Doctor, I need someone like you on my side, and I will do anything to ensure you remain safe."

Her words were solemn. He nodded in reply.

"Can she travel?" Francesca asked, reaching for her jacket.

"I don't think you have a choice," he said grimly. He handed her a black bag. "This has antibiotics and some other first-aid supplies that should help. If she isn't feeling better by tomorrow, she may need a blood transfusion."

"I'm taking her to a safe house in the mountains of Calabria. I can't take her to a hospital. They will ask questions. They will make connections."

"I understand." The doctor stood. "Good luck."

EPILOGUE

Capo Paci, Scilla, Italy

Eva stood in the window overlooking her spacious brick courtyard three stories below. All the windows were wide open, letting in a cool, salty ocean breeze laced with the smell of ripening lemons and blood oranges from the trees in her gardens.

The walled courtyard perched a hundred feet above the sea below. Eva had destroyed the brick stairs leading down to the water, creating a sheer face that only an expert rock climber could scale. And even if someone managed to make it to the top, they would trigger an alarm. The courtyard's walled sides were flanked by thick, closely planted rows of Italian cypress trees on each side to prevent the prying eyes of curious neighbors from seeing within.

Eva lifted her gaze out to the Tyrrhenian Sea—a turquoise blue for as far as she could see. Her homeland, Sicily, lay not far to the southwest. Sometimes she thought she could glimpse landfall on the horizon and imagined she was gazing on Palermo. Probably not. But it was enough to know it was there. Waiting. It would be there when she was ready to attack.

She surveyed her soldiers below fighting with longswords, rapiers, daggers, and dueling knives. All were women ranging in age from twenty to fifty. Handpicked for their grit, their physical prowess, their inner strength, their innate power. Their passion.

This class numbered twenty.

From her perch in her office, Eva watched the women train at least twice a day. They knew she was watching. It made them work harder. Occasionally, she'd catch one of them shooting a quick glance up to her lookout.

She studied their movements as they followed Catrina, her best trainer. The blonde Northern Italian stood in front of them, leading them in the sleek movements. A glint of silver flashed as the rows of black-clad, masked women parried and thrust and dipped as they learned the ancient martial art form of Gladiatura Moderna.

The women moved with precision. They were Deadly. Beautiful. Ruthless. Trained assassins. Loyal to the core. Of course, that loyalty would be tested. Those not capable of what Eva demanded were let go, though with a hefty severance package. Those who remained were treated as sisters and soon became a close-knit family. It wasn't a cult.

It was an army.

The hot sun beat down on her through the window. Eva pushed back the sleeve of her black blouse, revealing the tattoo snaking up her forearm: *La vendetta è mia*. Vengeance is mine.

One class had already graduated. They were her first pick—the ones she trusted with her life. They knew most, but not all, of her secrets. This new class would serve as her foot soldiers. They were more expendable. It was unfortunate, but necessary.

Eva had realized being a leader meant difficult choices at times. She'd studied all the greats for the past year—*The Art of War* by Sun Tzu, *The Persian Expedition* by Xenophon, and books on Napoleon, Alexander the Great, Winston Churchill, and Genghis Khan, among others. She knew what it would take to battle the powers that be—those remaining mob bosses who still refused to acknowledge as one of them.

Her battle was that of a stealth fighter. Already, the whispers were beginning.

The numerous bodies found with the Queen of Spades card upon them were striking fear into the hearts of her enemies. She knew that to win this war, she must first best them mentally. Besting them physically was the icing on the cake. If she struck fear into the enemy's soldiers, she'd already won.

It had begun.

Her surveillance was interrupted by a soft knock on her door.

Eva turned, facing the interior of her office. The walls were lined with bookshelves of dark wood, filled with colorful hardbacks and paperbacks. A massive black desk sat facing the sea with a red velvet upholstered chair pulled up to it. Between the desk and windows where Eva stood was a red velvet love seat where those she'd summoned could sit. Rather than take her seat at the desk, Eva remained standing. A second, coded knock—double rap followed by a single rap. Francesca. Her first—and most trusted—warrior.

After Francesca helped Eva escape and nursed her back to health, the two women had plotted the downfall of the rest of the Mafiosi and warned them—fuck with Eva's operations at their own peril. It took a few high-profile murders for Eva to convince the men she meant business.

"Enter."

The redheaded woman entered. Francesca wore tight black pants with combat boots and a black blazer over a black T-shirt. Her hair was pulled back in a long ponytail, her eyelids were painted gray with smoky makeup, and her lips painted petal pink. She was the most stunning sixty-five-year-old Eva had ever seen. And the smartest.

By the look on Francesca's face, Eva knew what her visit was about. Francesca had found the answers to the questions Eva had asked so long ago. It had happened shortly after the scene at Francesca's house. When she'd recovered she went to visit Palermo. She'd wanted to see it now that Mazzo was no longer in power.

As she walked through Palermo, surrounded by her guards, an older woman appeared out of nowhere in front of Eva on the empty sidewalk. She could not have been even four feet tall. Her features were mostly obscured by a black shawl over her head, but her eyes glittered knowingly out of a wrinkled face.

At first, Eva stepped into the street to give the woman the right-of-way, but the elder woman crooked a gnarled finger, drawing Eva close. The woman spoke, but it was a low rasp, so Eva dipped her head next to the woman's mouth so she could hear.

When she did, two of Eva's female bodyguards drew their swords, but Eva held up a palm and they retreated, scowling.

When the woman spoke again, her hot breath ruffling Eva's hair and sending chills down her neck as it met her ear, Eva could barely make out the words. When they finally sunk in, Eva drew back, her eyes wide. The woman had said, "You have a sister."

Eva was speechless. The woman nodded sagely and then shuffled off. Eva made to follow her, but one of her bodyguard's touched Eva's elbow and jutted her chin toward a black SUV crawling up the steep road. *Polizia.* Time to leave.

When Eva turned back, the woman had disappeared.

Back at the hideout on the mainland, Eva had immediately called Francesca into her study.

"I don't know if you have a sister, but I regret to inform you your mother passed last year."

Eva nodded slightly. She had assumed that. But still it hurt to hear it. Her face didn't reveal a thing.

"My half brothers shipped my mother off to Rome when I was a teenager. She was their stepmother. I never heard from her again," Eva said. "She may have been pregnant at the time."

"I will find out for you."

"Thank you."

Francesca bowed slightly. The two women had an interesting relationship. The older woman was Eva's most trusted advisor. But for some reason, Francesca, a force in our own right, deferred to Eva on all things.

Once, Eva had confronted her about it. "You should be a woman of honor. You should not be taking direction or orders from me."

"I am not a leader. I don't want to be a leader. What I want is to help you in your mission. I've thought long and hard about the best way for me to do that, and if you will so honor me, I ask to remain your consigliere."

In the Mafia, consigliere was the boss's right-hand man—in this case woman—their most trusted and close confidante and friend. They were the only ones within the entire structure who dared argue with the boss. Since Eva didn't trust anyone enough to have an underboss and Francesca would not accept that role, the redhead was second-in-command. Eva had even drawn up a will, leaving everything to Francesca if she died.

Eva searched the woman's eyes for a few seconds before nodding. "Please then. Please be my consigliere. It would be a tremendous honor."

"The honor is mine," Francesca said.

That night Eva transferred millions of dollars into the woman's bank account. She did it to thank Francesca, but also because it would ensure that Francesca remained loyal to her for all the right reasons. The transfer of money was never mentioned.

Now, in her private office, Eva turned to face the window again. She didn't want Francesca to see her expression as she received the news.

"I found her," Francesca said.

Eva didn't respond.

"Your mother gave birth to her when you were eight."

Eva felt her forehead scrunch together. She sat quietly for a few seconds and it came back to her in blurry snapshots. Her mother overweight, suddenly bulky in a housedress. Her father sending her mother to Rome to stay with Eva's aunt. When Eva complained her father said it was to keep her mother safe. Eva didn't question it. Decisions like that were made often in her household. Eva remembered the one time her father had raised his hand to her. She had been seven years old and had delivered a message for him and then fallen asleep in the hills. When she returned home he had slapped her. She had been mortified.

Her mother had patiently explained to Eva that the men their family did business with were very dangerous and would not hesitate to hurt a child to prove a point. Her father had been worried they'd done something to her.

The next day her father sent her to a small northern village for a month to learn the art of *Gladiatura Moderna*, the Italian martial arts style that primarily used weapons in a fighting style much like fencing. The weapons she learned to manipulate included medieval daggers, longswords, *liccasapuni*—long thin, Sicilian dueling knives, and even wooden walking sticks.

When she came back, her father told her she would continue her lessons three times a week with the local expert and that her mother was leaving for Rome for about four months.

That is when it must have happened, that is when her mother must've given birth to her sister, Eva realized now. She nodded at Francesca who continued.

"Your sister is alive and living in Monterey, California. Her name is Lucia-Grazia Santella."

Her shoulders sagged hearing the name. A sister. A blood relative. Named after her. Her emotions welled up in her throat. She would not cry. It was unseemly.

She waited. Francesca had more to say, apparently.

"Your sister is pregnant. With a boy. Due any day."

She was an aunt. Eva waited. She could tell by the way Francesca paused that there was still more.

"Your sister has another child. A fifteen-month-old daughter."

Eva closed her eyes, trying to stem the flood of tears threatening to breach the corners of her eyes.

"Name?" Her voice was hoarse, revealing her emotions ever so slightly. Eva held her breath, waiting. "What's the little girl's name?"

Finally, Francesca spoke:

"Giada Valentina Santella."

The story continues in *One-Eyed Jack*, next in the Queen of Spades Thriller Series. Head to the next page for a sneak peek or order today by scanning the QR code below!

Stay up to date with Kristi Belcamino's new releases by scanning the QR code below!

(You'll receive a **free** copy of *First Vengeance: A Gia Santella Prequel!*)

Did you enjoy *Queen of Spades?* Scan the QR code below to let us know your thoughts!

ONE-EYED JACK CHAPTER ONE

Eva Lucia Santella woke with her hands between her legs, panting and writhing in pleasure.

The brilliant, golden Italian sunshine lit up the white covers of her king-size bed. An ocean breeze lifted the filmy white curtains into the air. Her dark hair spilled out like ink over the silk pillow.

She'd been dreaming of her husband, Matthew. They had been making love on the beach in front of their Malibu home as the sun set. It had never happened in real life. Their stretch of beach wasn't private enough. But in her dream, they had the beach to themselves. The kids were... well, safe some-where...and she and Matthew were like horny teenagers as they fucked on the large cashmere blanket spread out on the sand. She buried her face into his neck and came wildly with abandon. As the orgasm melted away, the dream also began to dissolve.

Right before her long dark lashes fluttered open, Eva realized that she could still smell her husband. Hovering right between a dream state and consciousness, Eva could recall Matthew's smell as vividly as she felt the ocean breeze on her face.

In that moment, reality punched her in the gut like a fist. She sat up in bed and looked around, bewildered and feeling hollow inside. The emptiness of her massive bedroom was like a slap. There was no husband. No giggling kids running into the room to pile into bed with them on a Saturday morning, begging them to get up and make pancakes.

Her family was dead. They were all dead—buried in dark, cold graves across the ocean in America.

Eva shook off her grief and put it in a small, internal compartment to deal with later. As she stretched her arms above her in bed, she was already planning out her day—how she could avenge her family by destroying every last Mafia boss in Italy.

She'd taken a fatal swoop at some of them, killing a dozen at once, but there were more to go.

It was what got her out of bed every day.

It drove her to train and work out for hours at a time, honing her body into a lethal weapon. And now she had raised an army of women just like her. Even though the sun had only just risen, she could hear them in the courtyard below, training in the ancient Italian martial arts form of *Gladiatura Moderna*.

Throwing back her covers, she swung her legs around until her feet hit the cool marble floor. Time to conquer the day.

ONE-EYED JACK CHAPTER TWO

Downstairs, Eva squeezed a fresh lemon into a glass of water, fixed an espresso, and headed out to the stone patio through the large French doors with both drinks and her leather-bound journal and planner. Beyond her patio deck, she could see the turquoise blue of the Tyrrhenian sea stretched out for miles before her, sparkling in the early morning sunlight. She settled in at one of the café tables scattered on the patio and inhaled. She was surrounded by lemon trees, and their scent comingling with the salty sea was one of her favorite smells. Sipping her coffee, she opened her leather-bound journal to review her plans for the day.

After breakfast, she had a meeting with one of her more promising soldiers. The girl was just seventeen. She'd been recruited by Francesca, Eva's most trusted and loyal friend and business partner.

Francesca had found the girl as a runaway on the streets of Rome. Monica had fled an abusive stepfather in the countryside and was hoping to make a new life in the big city, but she had fallen in with the wrong crowd—a group of thieves and drug addicts who wanted to make her a prostitute.

Monica was about to have her first meeting with a "client" when Francesca had stepped in and offered her a new life. At first the girl scoffed, but then Francesca played her wild card—the girl would be working for, and *with*, the Queen of Spades. That was all it had taken.

Over the past two decades, Eva's nickname, her nomenclature, if you will, had become a legend in Sicily and Italy. Little girls played "Queen of Spades" and little boys pretended to marry her. She was the people's hero. She was known to take from the rich and give to the poor.

When Eva had been a mob boss, before the hit was placed on her life, she made sure her "people" were never without. She had earned their loyalty for life. Generations of children looked up to her. When the other Mafioso tried to kill her, she had to flee and disappeared to America. When she returned after a decade, nobody had forgotten. When word grew that she had slain twelve of the most vicious mob leaders and that she was back in Italy, there were parties and dancing in the streets for three days.

Today, after two months of training, Monica would meet Eva for the first time. Eva had kept a close eye on the girl from day one and had been pleased with the young woman's fiery spirit and adept physical prowess. This morning, Eva would offer her a leadership role. Each band of her small army had lieutenants in charge of their designated squads.

After that meeting, Eva had a phone call with her financial adviser. She had lived off her investments for years and still liked to monitor them weekly. This week, she was going to direct her adviser to donate half a million Euros to a women's shelter that had just opened in a southern Italian city, Bernalda.

Later, she had a lunch meeting planned with four of the most important businessmen in Southern Italy. They were going to discuss ways to bolster the Southern Italian economy. After lunch, Eva would work out for three hours before a late dinner with a visiting politician from Rome who said he needed her help financially. She would consider it. He had been active in fighting sex trafficking, something that was near and dear to Eva's heart. It had been her own refusal to engage in sex trafficking years ago that had started the war against her and led to the lifelong price on her head.

But before all of that, she had her most important meeting of the day—the one with Francesca. Her *consigliere*, as they said.

The red-haired, older woman arrived ten minutes later, swooping into the patio area with a massive mug of hot tea and a smile. She wore an ankle-length green silk Cheongsam dress, high wedge sandals, and her deep red hair was pulled back from her face with an emerald clip that still allowed it to flow down her back.

She looked like an Italian geisha, Eva thought as she rose to kiss her on both cheeks.

Once they were settled in at the table and sipping their drinks, Francesca took out her iPad.

"Something came in overnight."

Eva waited, but Francesca's tone had aroused her curiosity.

"From that website," Francesca said.

Eva stopped herself from rolling her eyes. It was unbecoming for a grown woman to do so.

"That website" was a fan site for the Queen of Spades.

The nickname had stuck after she'd become a notorious mob boss and assassin as a teenager. In Italy, the Queen of Spades playing card signified death. At first, she used the cards as a warning—such as "stop sex trafficking or you will die." And then it morphed into her calling card. Each time she killed, Eva left the playing card on the victim's body.

That life and world seemed so far away from where she sat now on the patio of the finest villa on her stretch of Italian coastline. So much had happened since then.

Now, when people, especially Americans, thought of the Queen of Spades, they thought of an avenging warrior who would rectify dangerous child custody issues. It had started innocently enough—helping out her friend Jonathan's friend—but then more and more people had reached out to her for help.

When she complained to Jonathan that the international flights to America were expensive, he'd offered to cash out his 401K to pay for them. Touché. They both knew her wealth made that a nonissue.

"Baby, I have other priorities," she told him. "I'm raising an army over here. I have to take down the *Cosa Nostra*. I'm playing a bigger game here— what you over there would consider the Super Bowl."

"Yeah, yeah, nice sports analogy, and good for you," he'd say and hang up. Then he'd text her pictures of the kid in an emergency room with a broken arm or the mother with a black eye and stitches across her cheek.

Dirty pool. It always worked.

In his defense, Jonathan was careful that only the really hard luck cases were brought to her attention. The ones where the abusive parent was so powerful or connected that the other spouse could not turn to lawful resources to save their kids.

So far, Eva had helped a dozen parents with these types of custody disputes. Reluctantly, at first, but then she was always glad when it was over.

The idea that a fan site had sprung up from these actions was baffling for Eva to think about. As soon as it had, Jonathan had contacted the creator. When he told the person privately that he knew the Queen of Spades, he'd been made an administrator.

"What is it this time?" Eva finally said to Francesca.

"A private message for you on the site. Jonathan said to forward it to you as soon as possible."

Eva closed her eyes for a second. As much as she hated the idea of the site, a part of her knew that her work in America was part of her healing process. Helping others was actually helping herself and her own gut-wrenching, heart-stabbing grief. She even sometimes snuck onto the site to read the posts and, every once in a while, seeing that she really had helped other people helped to temporarily numb the grief of her own tragedy.

But she would die before she admitted to Francesca she'd ever even been on the site.

In any case, she wasn't privy to private messages.

Francesca logged on to Jonathan's account and pushed the iPad over to Eva to read.

When she finished, Eva sat back. The letter was unnerving, hinting at a mass murder in a few weeks. But the details were sparse. And who was the One-Eyed Jack?

When she looked up, Francesca met her eyes.

"Jonathan said he immediately forwarded this to the FBI and the police but nobody seems to be taking him seriously. Their response was for him to call back when there were more details."

"Lovely," Eva said. Her voice dripped sarcasm. As a woman wanted by law enforcement in America for a crime she didn't commit, she didn't have a lot of faith in their abilities.

"Traced him to some pretty offensive websites," Francesca said. "The content and motive of these groups he's in is quite alarming.

"Oh yeah?"

"Have you heard of incels?"

Eva shook her head. She gestured to the iPad. "First time I heard the word was in this letter."

Francesca gave her a look. "It's distasteful to speak of over breakfast."

Eva stood. "Let's take a walk. You can tell me all about it. We'll eat after."

They walked down on the beach below the villa and its high stone walls. By the time they got to the rocky outcrop that ended that particular stretch of beach, Francesca had finished.

The gist of it was that there were apparently as many as 60,000 people in online forums spewing hatred against women. They all identified themselves as "incels" which loosely meant they were involuntarily celibate.

A few of them, including a California man named Elliot Rodger, had gone off the rails for their "cause," by deciding to express his frustration through mass murder. Rodger, twenty-two, wrote a 140-page manifesto against women and then killed six people before killing himself.

He'd become an incel hero. People referred to him as ER and spoke of "pulling an ER" as committing a mass shooting.

Rodger left behind several videos, including one that spoke of his revenge murders saying, "I will slaughter every single spoiled stuck-up blonde slut."

But he wasn't the only incel that took on a kamikaze mass shooting mission according to Francesca. A Pittsburg man killed three women in an aerobics class before killing himself, and a Toronto man, claiming to be starting the 'Incel Rebellion' mowed down ten pedestrians in his van.

A few other incels who spoke publicly about their mass shooting plans had been stopped in time.

"They have their own jargon," Francesca said. "Chad and Alphas are men who easily attract women. Women who are attractive enough to date anyone are Stacy's. And ER simply acknowledges Elliot Rodger and his martyr status. They also call him Saint Elliot."

"Jesus Christ," Eva said.

The evil in the world would never cease. Eva had seen more of it first-hand than most families do in several generations.

The two women paused at the end of the beach, staring out toward Sicily —their homeland and the headquarters of their shared enemy—the *Cosa Nostra*.

Eva kept her expression unreadable.

After a few seconds, she asked, "What big events are planned in Florida next month?"

"Several," Francesca said as they turned back toward the stone steps leading to the villa gate. "But three large ones that involve women specifically. The Miss America pageant, a Women's March against the U.S. President, and a BellaDonna Convention."

Eva raised an eyebrow at the last one.

"It's a cosmetics company in the U.S. Home parties and sales and such. Supposed to be really good quality too. Making millionaires left and right."

"Brava," Eva said. "These three events? Are they all in different cities?" Eva asked.

Francesca shook her head. "That might be the only break we have. Or maybe it will make it worse, I don't know. They are all in Miami and all the same weekend. Next week."

Eva squared her shoulders. When Francesca saw this, she said, "I'll make sure everything here is under control while you're gone."

Eva smiled for the first time since they'd left the villa.

"Francesca, you are a queen. I have no idea why you stick around."

Are you loving *One-Eyed Jack?* Order your copy today by scanning the QR code below!

ALSO BY KRISTI BELCAMINO

Enjoying Kristi Belcamino? Scan the QR code below to see her Amazon Author page!

Gia Santella Crime Thriller Series

Vendetta

Vigilante

Vengeance

Black Widow

Day of the Dead

Border Line

Night Fall

Stone Cold

Cold as Death

Cold Blooded

Dark Shadows

Dark Vengeance

Dark Justice

Deadly Justice

Deadly Lies

Additional books in series:

Taste of Vengeance

Lone Raven

Vigilante Crime Series

Blood & Roses

Blood & Fire

Blood & Bone

Blood & Tears

Queen of Spades Thrillers

Queen of Spades

The One-Eyed Jack

The Suicide King

The Ace of Clubs

The Joker

The Wild Card

High Stakes

Poker Face

Standalone Novels

Coming For You

Sanctuary City

The Girl in the River

Buried Secrets

Dead Wrong (Young Adult Mystery)

ALSO BY WITHOUT WARRANT

More Thriller Series from Without Warrant Authors

Dana Gray Mysteries by C.J. Cross

Girl Left Behind

Girl on the Hill

Girl in the Grave

The Kenzie Gilmore Series by Biba Pearce

Afterburn

Dead Heat

Heatwave

Burnout

Deep Heat

Fever Pitch

Storm Surge

Willow Grace FBI Thrillers

by Without Warrant and C. C. West

Shadow of Grace

Condition of Grace

Hunt for Grace

Time for Grace

Piece of Grace

Gia Santella Crime Thriller Series

by Kristi Belcamino

Vendetta

Vigilante

Vengeance

Black Widow

Day of the Dead

Border Line

Night Fall

Stone Cold

Cold as Death

Cold Blooded

Dark Shadows

Dark Vengeance

Dark Justice

Deadly Justice

Deadly Lies

Vigilante Crime Series by Kristi Belcamino

Blood & Roses

Blood & Fire

Blood & Bone

Blood & Tears

Queen of Spades Thrillers by Kristi Belcamino

Queen of Spades

The One-Eyed Jack

The Suicide King

The Ace of Clubs

The Joker

The Wild Card

High Stakes

Poker Face

AUTHOR'S NOTE

When I was 16, I read Jackie Collins' book, *Lucky*, and it rocked my world. For the first time in my prolific reading life (yes, I was the kid holed up in my room reading as many books as I could as often as I could), I met a character who was not only Italian-American like me, but a strong, powerful, and successful badass woman who didn't take crap from anybody and loved to have sex!

Although I had dreamed of being a writer, it never seemed like a realistic dream and my attempts at writing seemed pitiful. So I studied journalism and became a reporter—it was a way to be a writer and have a steady paycheck.

It was only when I was in my forties that I got the guts to write a book. And it was a few years after that I was brave enough to write the characters I really wanted to write—Gia Santella, Eva Santella and Rose.

If you like these women, I'm pretty sure we'd be the best of friends in real life!

x Kristi

ABOUT THE AUTHOR

Kristi Belcamino is a USA Today bestseller, an Agatha, Anthony, Barry & Macavity finalist, and an Italian Mama who bakes a tasty biscotti.

Her books feature strong, kickass, independent women facing unspeakable evil in order to seek justice for those unable to do so themselves.

In her former life, as an award-winning crime reporter at newspapers in California, she flew over Big Sur in an FA-18 jet with the Blue Angels, raced a Dodge Viper at Laguna Seca, attended barbecues at the morgue, and conversed with serial killers.

During her decade covering crime, Belcamino wrote and reported about many high-profile cases including the Laci Peterson murder and Chandra Levy disappearance. She has appeared on *Inside Edition* and local television shows. She now writes fiction and works part-time as a reporter covering the police beat for the St. Paul *Pioneer Press*.

Her work has appeared in such prominent publications as *Salon*, the *Miami Herald, San Jose Mercury News,* and *Chicago Tribune.*

facebook.com/kristibelcaminowriter

instagram.com/kristibelcaminobooks

tiktok.com/@kristibelcaminobooks

Made in the USA
Monee, IL
09 May 2024

58222236R00115